AND THE WOLF SHALL DWELL

AND THE WOLF SHALL DWELL

JONI DEE

Blue Poppy Publishing

Copyright © 2017

The right of Yonathan Dital to be identified as the author of this work has been asserted.
All rights reserved. This book or any portion thereof may not be reproduced or used in any manner whatsoever without the express written permission of the Publisher and Author except for the use of brief quotations in a book review.

This is a work of fiction. Names, characters, businesses, places, events and incidents are either the products of the author's imagination or used in a fictitious manner. Any resemblance to actual persons, living or dead, or actual events is purely coincidental.

Cover art by Omer Sagiv Studio omersagiv.com

Author website – jondbooks.com
Blue Poppy Publishing logo is a registered trademark.
All rights reserved.

Published by Blue Poppy Publishing, Devon
EX34 9HG info@bluepoppypublishing.co.uk

2nd Edition

ISBN-13 : 978-1-911438-23-6

For my children,

in memory of your great-grandma

Dvora Shalem.

An amazing woman who would have urged

you to always aim for the stars!

Book I

Chapter 1
John

5 am. Gracechurch Avenue's lamp posts had managed a feeble attempt to chase away the darkness left by the night, but it still refused to give way to the rising dawn. The temperature was freezing cold, and the grey-bluish night mist seemed to absorb the lamp posts' dim orange light.

Had he not known what time it was, John could have sworn it was still the middle of the night, rather than morning. The sun was a late riser in London these days, as if she was aching for a lie-in herself, preferring the warmth of a pampering goose down duvet to spreading some light onto the frozen street.

John, back home called Yochi – an abbreviation for Yochanan, had to make his way to the office in the early morning hours, so that he would start his working day alongside the overseas offices of his employer's company.

Today, he left his soulless Tower Bridge serviced apartment, which was rented for him by the firm, even before the clock struck five. It was his sixth month in the kingdom's capital, a gig which had started as a temporary project assignment, and subsequently took shape as a rather permanent posting to the firm's London offices. And yet, he didn't mind. At thirty winters old, John – single and unattached – was happy to spend time in one of the world's most buzzing cultural cities. It sure as hell beat the provinciality of back home.

John was unmistakably a handsome man. He was six foot tall, and had an upright and self-confident posture, which was not apparent under his oafish black winter coat. His brown hair was mostly hidden under the black beanie hat he wore only until he was to reach the office, just at the end of Liverpool Street station. Despite his relatively young age, John's face was already etched with a hint of some wrinkles, especially beneath his big, olive coloured eyes. He yawned; his fatigue was a direct outcome of the numerous working hours he was putting in (along with the drinking nights with the British colleagues).

He picked up his pace, stepping over the large, crooked, cobblestone pavement, going past the lorry drivers and the merchants who were unloading at the entrance to Leadenhall market. These were the first signs that Wednesday had begun, though for John yesterday had never truly ended. He had been up all night running different scenarios in his head for a possible failure of the computer program he had been working on for the past months.

John's firm was situated in the east end of the City of London, right by the big banks and brokerage firms. This location was not coincidental, as his firm was developing online trading and banking applications for exactly this clientele base. Today's software launch would determine John's future with the firm. Success meant prestige, an assured continuation of the London based project and a nice five figure incentive bonus; whereas failure would most likely send him to the unemployment office back home.

The pavement felt rough under his frozen feet, and he stumbled as the path curved to the left. A refuse truck pulled up beside him, and burly workers, dressed in bright yellow jumpers, nearly ran over him on their way to the big dumpster bins of the crossroads, where the avenue becomes Bishopsgate. The commotion they caused woke him up, sharpened his senses, and he picked up his pace in order to keep warm and maybe also to distract the pessimistic notions regarding his project.

As he reached the gargantuan building of Liverpool Street station, he took out a pack of cigarettes and lingered at the entrance. He never used to smoke before midday, but since he was up for already a day and a half, he figured he could get away with it. The warm smoke engulfed his cold lungs and made his throat tingle. He felt dizzy and after three more puffs, threw the cigarette to the kerb.

Walking on the lower level of the station was his best route to reach the company's offices in Broadgate Circle, at the end of the station. Plus, the sheltered station provided some protection from the chilly outdoors. Despite the hour, a few people were already waiting for the early trains, and on a warmer day he would have gladly avoided the hubbub and overtaken the station from outside. At these hours he was still not accustomed to interacting, no – he was not a morning person at all. It was only with the triple-shot espresso he would drink in about an hour's time that his hostility towards the world would start to dissolve.

"STOP! WE JUST WANT TO TALK TO YOU!" A shout was heard through the dozens of people standing in the station. Everybody immediately turned their gaze towards the source of the cry and started moving uncomfortably to either clear the way or to locate the person responsible for the racket.

Abruptly, an elderly man emerged from in-between the crowd, running frantically towards John. He ran into a young man's shoulder and kept the forward charge while pushing another woman and mumbling apologetic words. He was wearing a brown suit with a tweed jacket that had seen better days. His skin looked clammy, a result of his overwrought run.

The old man's eyes were darting around, and he had a panicky look on his face. His eyes were trying to focus on something that seemed not there, rather than concentrating on finding a safe route between the people. John was transfixed. Like a deer staring into the lights of a vehicle at night he was unable to move aside as the man picked up his run and headed straight towards him. The collision was inevitable.

With a loud thud John fell to the ground with the man lying on top of him.

"I am sorry... I am sorry," cried the old man, trying to pick himself up from John, neither seeking nor being offered any help from the bystanders. In the corner of his eye, John saw two men, dressed in black leather jackets, heading towards them. His first thought was that their coats were too thin for the cold weather, as if they were meant to impress rather than to actually provide warmth to their owners. He immediately dismissed the thought as irrelevant and lifted himself while aiding the man to his feet.

"The Queen... the Queen... where she is seated... they are all standing there behind her." John gave a baffled stare to the man, who seemed incoherent and spoke with a foreign, maybe east European accent. "THE QUEEN – come on – they are all standing!" he begged, as his eyes shot a penetrating stare into John's.

As the leathered gentlemen drew near, the man shot off again and John thought he heard him mumble, "Remember the Queen." While one of the chasers reached John, the other kept running after the old man. He touched John's shoulder and straightened his coat, gently frisking him as if he was looking for a weapon of some sort.

"You okay, mate?" the pursuer asked, though something about his smile seemed phony, or at least insincere. Meanwhile the elderly man ran through an open gate to the train platform. John was still shaken and before he could begin to answer, a shriek was heard throughout the station's hall.

The screeching noise of a train applying its brakes filled the air and scorched John's eardrums. More screams were now heard and a toddler started crying. Dozens of people started to run towards the platform, where the man had thrown himself before the oncoming train, which was just arriving at platform two.

"Did he hand you anything?" the man asked John abruptly and with annoyance.

"Huh?" John was focused on the commotion and missed the question.

"The old man!" The man's voice was sharp. "Did he give you anything?"

"No," John stammered. "I mean, I don't think so… he just knocked me over." He found it hard to compose himself.

The man drew out a business card and stuffed it into John's palm. "Give me a call if you remember anything—" he spoke in a raggedy cockney accent, and never mentioned his name "—just a mad geezer, hey mate?!" The man's smile was broad and seemed inappropriate.

He disengaged and headed rapidly towards the escalator leading to the top floor of the station, signalling his friend as they both made their way away from the scene of the incident. Met and Transport police officers were already congregating near the platforms.

"Yes…" John murmured, but the guy was long gone.

Chapter 2
Grey

The alarm clock went off with an old metallic ring and woke him from a dream that now he had trouble remembering. He looked through his bedroom's bay window. It was 6 am, and the London morning was bluish-grey with no sign of the sun, still hiding behind the horizon.

He got up and went into the bathroom. He washed his face, put on his glasses and studied his own reflection. A middle-aged man, greying hair with a hint of its former brown, and deep wrinkles around his bright blue eyes. Even at fifty-five, Adam Grey was still a handsome man, who used his charm for constant nightly conquests. Yesterday was not one of those nights; in fact he had found it hard to sleep for all the wrong reasons.

He briskly brushed his teeth and shaved. He put on a deep blue pinstripe suit over a white-and-blue plaid dress shirt which he fitted with a pair of gold cufflinks. He tied a dark grey tie in a double Windsor knot – learned at Eton – and finished the look with a dark grey handkerchief folded into a perfect triangle and slid into the suit's breast pocket. Whenever he tied a tie he remembered his old all-boys' school. Between the useless classes and the cricket games, the lectures and the banter, the image of the omnipotent Headmaster Crouch's constant shouting was the one memory that stood out the most. 'Grey! If Windsor Castle were to be built the way you tie your Windsor...' he never did finish the sentence.

Grey wondered what Headmaster Crouch was doing today. Probably in some nursing home, if still alive. He shook the thought away.

Closing the front door behind him and heading south towards Sloane Square, Grey surveyed the familiar Georgian-Victorian Street. His three-storey house gleamed brightly white in contrast to the sombre English day. He and his brother had inherited the house when their parents passed away. They split it into a two-flat conversion, three bedrooms each. His brother sold his flat a long time ago, and Grey had to cope with living alongside a family of Turks, with their two boisterous children who insisted upon playing ball indoors. He sighed.

His walk along Chester Street was uneventful. It had been five years since Grey retired from the service. There was something eerie about breaking his retirement routine: a daily jog starting at Eaton Park going all the way to Hyde Park, then a Tube ride back, a shower, and brunch at Thomas Cubitt, a bar restaurant located half a block from his flat. Not today.

Grey entered Sloane Square and crossed the road in front of the Peter Jones department store, took a left turn and entered the Underground station. He walked down the steps leading to the platform, and waited for the east-bound train. The number of people on the platforms at this hour was ridiculous, he thought, all heading towards the City in an obsessive pursuit of money that would bring them neither joy nor happiness. While waiting on the platform to board the next train, he still had a troubling notion at the back of his head, left by yesterday's events.

Yesterday, at exactly 5 pm, the phone's pitchy ring sliced through the air of his Elizabeth Street flat. After three rings it went silent, and Grey, who was just coming from the kitchen where he had been waiting for the kettle to boil, presumed he simply had not reached it on time. As he went back to the kitchen, the phone rang again once and went dead. This made him anxious; he immediately recognized this pattern of rings for a familiar code from his days in the service. The first thought that went through his head was that it must be someone from days of yore, who believed Grey to be still serving in active duty. But who? And why now? He knew that unless he rang a prearranged number in a short predetermined period of time, he might never know the answer.

He picked up the phone and dialled a familiar number.

"Operator. State your business please," a man said on the other end of the line.

"Grey. Triple five – two – one – eight."

"Please hold, sir."

A few moments later, a young man answered the call.

"Good evening, Mr Grey. Were the old golf courses booked solid today?"

"Funny, kid. What's your name?"

"Potter. Roger Potter, sir."

"Listen up, Potter." Grey heard the young man swallow hard at the other end of the line. "I just received a code that hasn't been used since the eighties – three rings. Then a precisely one-minute interval – then one ring."

"Mmmm—"

"Please find out if there's an active protocol with this code with this number and any of my old cases as cross reference, and if there is – give me the call-back number. We need to call it asap."

"I am not sure it is within my privilege to give out this information – should it even exist, Mr Grey."

"Listen, kid, normally there are about thirty minutes to place the return call, or the agent is instructed to disengage any further contact. I have no desire to ever return to active duty, but if you want to stay in one, I suggest you find me the number so I can check the matter, and report back to you."

"Okay, please hold, sir."

Full five minutes had passed until Finch, the on-duty officer, took charge and got on the line. He was far friendlier than Potter, probably remembering Grey from his days in the service. Finch gave Grey the number to a phone box in the Tower Hill area, and suggested that they had only roughly twenty minutes to call back. Finch added, "I had to manually look into your old files to locate the number, hence the delay. This is a protocol that was last used more than twenty-five years ago. Whoever this is, they must want you specifically, otherwise they would have used far more conventional methods of getting in touch. I am arranging a guest pass for you to come to Babylon tomorrow morning. I want you to schedule a meeting with this source for tomorrow, then head here straight after, for debriefing. We will pick it up from there. It's a new world here, Grey – it took balls and nerves of steel to entertain old agents – the service doesn't have what it takes for that nowadays."

The train seemed to Grey like a humongous plastic worm – squeezing into the platform space like toothpaste out of a tube. He just barely managed to get into the crowded carriage, which was stuffy and hot. His black wool overcoat only added to the airlessness feeling.

And the Wolf Shall Dwell

To make the call yesterday, Grey had gone down to an old phone box located just by his house on Elizabeth Street. It had been quite a while since he last placed a call from one of these things, which were a very sought after commodity in the eighties and nineties, the prehistoric era – before mobile phones. Standing in one that was serving most probably as a urinal for the local tramps, he swallowed hard, shoved a twenty pence coin into the slot and dialled the number Finch had given him. He didn't need pen and paper to memorize a few numbers. Still got it.

As the Tube made its way through the stations, with only a few stops to go, Grey recalled the conversation that had sent him on his way today.

"Murray, is that you?"

"Yes. Who is this?"

The voice was old. Old yet familiar.

"Ephraim."

Ephraim. It was the code name for an agent Grey knew long ago. It was 1982. Grey was a young lad just coming back from a simple posting in Eastern Europe. The lack of sufficient human resources, and an exposed mole in the service that had done considerable damage, meant that Grey was getting – at his young age – the responsibility for running all the agents in the Greater London area. It was the swansong of the old espionage game, or so it seemed, as the technology got better – it was the SIGINT professionals that got the resources and the attention of the brass upstairs. With nobody left who really cared, young agents like Grey got their chance on some good old fashioned spying games. He remembered Ephraim well. He remembered all his men. Ephraim's real name was Henry Haft, a mid-grade consular worker at the Polish commission. Grey calculated swiftly that

Haft had to be over eighty years old now, and to the best of his knowledge, was never 'made'.

"What is it, Henry?" Grey sounded impatient. He had used his real name. He had no patience for nostalgic agents. "I thought we were both retired," he added. "Why are you calling me? Why not contact the service directly?"

"Your service is rotten, it is part of it. Everything else is immaterial now, Mr Murray." Murray. It was one of many forgotten aliases that Grey once used. "Listen to me," Ephraim continued with a deep Polish accent that had not subsided despite years and years of living among the English. His voice sounded exhausted and weak. "I have to meet with you urgently. I've prepared a dossier for you, it's with me. You and you alone I can trust. Tomorrow. 7 am, Liverpool Street station, I will be sitting in a free-house, what you lot refer to as a pub, called the Merchant, with a copy of The *Times*. Keep clear if the newspaper isn't open."

Grey was almost speechless. He started to say something, and then stopped.

"Murray, you would want to see this." Haft had sensed his reluctance.

There were four missed calls on his phone display as he emerged from the Tube at Liverpool Street station. He dialled the number.

"Operator."

"Grey. Triple five – two – one –eight."

"One second, please."

The line went silent and a man picked up.

"Grey?"

"In the flesh."

"It's Finch. That number that tried reaching you yesterday—"

"An old source. I doubt it is of any interes—"

"Henry Haft?"

"How did you know?" Grey was on his toes.

"He jumped to his death in front of a train in Liverpool Street station about an hour ago. The police are at the scene."

Grey was silent. This was shocking. Had the old man truly come across something of value and as a result found his death? Back in the old days, assassinations were made to look like accidents or suicides on a regular basis. Ephraim's words set heavy in his mind: 'Your service is rotten, it is part of it'. A chill went through his spine.

"Grey? Are you there?"

"Yes," he almost whispered.

"There's a police officer in the station waiting to brief one of ours. Should I send Potter?"

"I am there. I'll handle this."

* * *

It was supposed to be a triumphant day. The software had been branded a theoretical success, with just a few minor bugs that could be handled by the outsourced team in Romania. Eran, his mate from the local office's IT department, confirmed that management was very happy with John, and that the London posting was not in any danger, so far.

Having no direct manager in the London office was a pure advantage. John could easily play hooky when he wanted, and today was a great opportunity to exercise that privilege, since he couldn't let his mind rest from this morning's events. As he was walking along Old Broad Street, heading towards the Bank of England, he felt the chill of the British winter penetrating his bones. 'The Queen… where she is seated… they are all standing there behind her'. Was it some sort of incoherent prophecy? He couldn't give this sentence a rest; it made no sense at all. The papers' websites had already branded the incident 'A suicide in a Tube station', and there were no words written about the two pursuers that had frightened the old man, a fact that seemed most peculiar to John, especially knowing how the tabloids loved to give as many details as possible when death was involved.

He entered the big round hall of the Royal Exchange building. What used to be the centre of the British financial system was now no more than a posh, high-end shopping mall, with a bar in its centre. It was grand and luxurious with boutique shops like Tiffany and Bvlgari around it. He greeted the tall French waiter, with whom he was friendly from before, sat on a stool by the bar, and ordered a Bloody Mary.

Meanwhile, Adam Grey was walking slowly along a small passage off London Wall. The police debriefing had been utterly useless. The CCTV in the station did not have footage of the incident; strangely enough it seemed to have stopped recording earlier this morning. The young Met officer was more than glad to officially hand the case over to the service, and Grey – having presented himself as from Scotland Yard – had to call the operator again so this could be verified, in case of inquiry. He then received a call from an Inspector Matthews, the shadow Yard person assigned to the case, who offered help in any means possible. That was a courtesy call, and Grey was all too familiar with such things. *That which hath been is that which shall be, and that which hath been done is that which shall be done; and there is nothing new under the sun.* He remembered the old Ecclesiastes proverb, which if his memory served him right was repeated by Ephraim on numerous occasions. A shiver went up and down his spine.

Debriefing TfL (Transport for London) workers was far more fruitful. A tall black guy called Mitchell, who had been stationed near the south entrance to the Tube, had managed to see the entire scene. He gave a description of the two chasers. Mitchell also described a young fellow, who had contact with the deceased man. A look into the CCTV from the cameras outside the station, a use of the Yard's identification programs, courtesy of Inspector Matthews, and a match was found. Yochanan Daniel, currently employed with a tier-two working permit visa. All the details showed that the company paying for his visa was just around the corner, and indeed, a brief chat with his co-workers at AlgoTrade advised Grey to check either the guy's serviced apartment near Tower Hill, or the Royal Exchange bar, where he could be found when he was bunking off. Grey's gut feeling pointed to the bar.

Grey entered the grand space of the Royal Exchange. The round bar was placed in the middle of the big hall, and around it were dozens of wooden stools, but only a few were occupied, as were the tables scattered around the bar.

Grey moved the chair that was to John's right, and addressed the barman, "House whisky, one cube. Thanks."

John glanced at him.

"I suppose it's a bit early for whisky." He smiled at John. "But I've had a rough day, you see, I saw a man killed this morning – just there in the station."

John raised his eyebrows in bewilderment. But remained silent.

"I suppose you had a rough morning as well." He pointed to the nearly empty glass of Bloody Mary in front of John.

"I saw the same thing," he mumbled, and downed the remainder of his drink with a brisk movement.

"That's exactly what I wanted to talk to you about, Mr Daniel."

John's slight apathy quickly changed into pure outrage. "Who are you? How do you know my name?" he protested.

"Easy now, I am one of the good guys," Grey said, keeping his deep tone calm. He had miles and miles of interviews and debriefing behind him, he knew every trick in the book, and yet he decided that with Mr Daniel, the direct approach would be the best. It was a gut instinct, and they usually paid off. "I didn't actually see the incident. I was assigned to investigate from Scotland Yard, as the reports I have received were inconsistent with a mere suicide. I also have a bit of a personal stake – let's call it that – in the matter."

"You knew the guy?" John asked.

"Yes," he hesitantly answered.

John felt a little relieved. He thought that the case had been signed, sealed and delivered to the public as a simple incident, as if a drunk tramp had fallen in the Tube or off London Bridge. He would happily cooperate if he thought this would help shed some light on the matter, but he didn't really know what to make of this morning's events, nor of the brief conversation he'd had with the man, if one can even refer to it as such.

"I had a report stating you had direct contact with the man," Grey continued. "Can you tell me in your own words what happened?"

"He was being chased," John answered.

Grey took a heavy sip from his whisky, put down the glass and produced a ten pound note from his wallet. "I think we'd better go somewhere more private."

Chapter 3
The Counting House

The inside of the Counting House was huge. It was still a typical British pub, with a mahogany wooden bar, only here it was placed in the centre of the big space, a setup much like in the bar they had left. The furniture was generally made out of dark red wood, giving the place a gloomy ambience. Grey came to their table with two pints of lager and as he handed one to John he nearly knocked over an old style green lamp, one of several which were placed on the tables. The place was not packed at 2.30 pm, but it was still more buzzing than the posh Royal Exchange.

"They claimed to be the police, well, they never claimed but that was the general notion… he, erm… gave me a card that says he is police, but he never said it outright." He dug in a coat pocket and produced a white business card, and placed it on the wooden table. Grey picked it up. It read 'Inspector Moore: Special Investigations Unit'. There was a small Met Police logo, and a phone number. Grey took out his mobile phone and dialled the number.

"Operator. State your business," a familiar voice said from the other end of the line.

Grey knew that police officers don't leave obscure business cards, and that the City of London's CCTV footage doesn't erase itself… he had a hunch, and the more he thought about it the more it looked as if the service's handprint was smeared all over this 'incident'. *Your service is rotten, it is part of it.*

"Grey. Triple five – two – one – eight. Get me Finch."

Deep in his heart he hoped the operator would be ignorant as per his request. But the all too familiar words followed:

"Please hold, sir."

He got up from the table, signalling to John with his finger to hold on, and walked a few paces towards an empty corner.

"Finch here."

"It's me."

"Are you using the informants' hotline?"

"Apparently…"

"Care to elaborate?"

"Well, I just dialled a number on a business card left for one of the witnesses at the scene where Ephraim was *killed*."

"By whom?!" he was genuinely surprised.

"Check in the system an alias of Inspector Moore. Tell me which directorate uses it."

"Hold on." His keyboard typing could be heard through the line. "Okay got it. Finish up and come in asap; we'll see if we can make any sense of it all."

Grey hung up. He went back to the table and nearly downed the rest of his pint. John sensed the anxiety that the older man felt. "Trouble in paradise, Mr Grey?" He took a sip from his own glass. It was an awkward question. Grey didn't know how much the young gentleman had overheard.

"Listen, kid, I don't know who this so-called Inspector Moore is and what his business is, but the guy who died was an informant of mine. We worked together for over ten years back in the day. So…" He sighed. "If there's anything else you know that can help me get to the bottom of this, I… I'd appreciate it."

John looked into the blue eyes of the middle-aged man. He looked well, even too well for his age, but his eyes reflected fatigue and exhaustion. The wrinkles on his face, on second glance, seemed as if they are a result of miles and miles of tension and worries. Yet underneath it all, the eyes looked sincere and there was something in his face that made John trust him, almost instinctively. Years of practising fakeness? John doubted it and yet was not sure he should share with Grey the old man's final words… Are indistinctive words, said while in flight, worth mentioning? It seemed farfetched and John decided against it.

"There's nothing else I can think of, Mr Grey," John answered. "He mumbled something but it was incoherent, there's nothing else."

"I see."

"Can I trust you, Mr Grey?" John asked, as if the question shot itself straight from his hip, without getting filtered by any good manners or tact. He was like that sometimes. "I mean… For heaven's sake! These men… they are from the same organization as you are!" he exclaimed.

Grey nodded.

"True, they looked young and erm… unlike you, inexperienced, but…" He lost his line of thought.

"They were rash enough to make an eighty-year-old man jump to his death." He completed the young man's sentence.

"Yes. Exactly."

"You can trust me, Yo-ka-nan," he struggled with the name. "I will find whoever did this."

"John. Call me John. Everyone else around here does."

"Okay, John."

"He did tell me something, Grey." He was upset with himself for actually blurting this out, after already settling the matter.

"This Inspector Moore?"

"No… I mean… him too, but I meant the old man."

"What was it?"

"It will sound silly, I don't really know what to make of it, something about the Queen standing or actually sitting, where everyone else is standing."

Grey raised his eyebrows. "Some sort of code?"

"I doubt it, he sounded genuinely disoriented. Does it make any sense to you?"

"No."

"Well, that's all I've got."

***

Grey stood outside at the busy crossroads of the Bank of England, waiting to pull over a cab. The conversation left him distraught. He gave John Daniel his mobile phone number in case he recalled anything else, but his intuition told him that the guy was telling it like it was, and there wasn't a single lead left for him to follow. His only hope was Finch with some internal inquiry that will most likely hit 'Chinese walls' and will be dismissed on the grounds of some bullshit excuse for secrecy.

He climbed into a cab that pulled over, and tried to reflect on the old man's last words, as John described them. Surely he'd got it wrong; Ephraim was never the one to engage in cryptography, he was a straight to the point guy. It was simply unthinkable that in his age the old dog started to learn some new tricks.

"Oy! Where to?" called the driver, probably for the third or fourth time.

"Sorry, mate, I must have been daydreaming. Right off Vauxhall Bridge, hmmm… it's 85 Prince Albert Embankment, Babylon-on-Thames." The taxi soared off.

***

Something didn't add up. He decided to head back to Liverpool Street station, even though he could have easily walked through Threadneedle Street straight to his apartment. He had no intention of returning to work today.

Walking along Old Broad Street portrayed the same old 'city scenario': busy pubs, restaurants, shoe repair shops that also cut keys, dry-cleaners, clothing shops and a 'Snappy Snap' photography shop that had the Queen's portrait hanging on the front door.

Where the Queen is seated. The portrait, taken by David Dawson, was a famous one. Showing Her Majesty Queen Elizabeth II wearing her jewelled crown. The photographer took the picture while he was an assistant to the famous painter Lucien Freud, who was busy distorting the Queen's features for his art, painting her in a twisted and macabre way – like most of his work. John increased his pace and nearly ran to the sheltered inside of the station. 'There are pictures of the Queen everywhere in this country' – it all became crystal clear to him.

He halted approximately where the old man bumped into him and tried to catch his breath. He began tracking back to the starting point of the man's run that ended with their collision. He walked past the big Boots pharmacy and stopped. This was the route he had taken each day; he already knew she would be there.

Exactly in a shooting distance from where people stood and looked up at the train departure board, was a gift and card shop set in a glass cubicle. The portrait of the Queen was there, on the wall of the shop, gazing statically at the commuters.

He managed to pretend that he was checking some cards, and spotted a brown Jiffy envelope stuffed right behind the card stand that was underneath the portrait. He slipped away, envelope in hand, right under the nose of the saleswoman, who was busy taking payment from a customer. He walked out of the station and into the cold, dry afternoon.

Chapter 4
Babylon-on-Thames

The SIS building's sixth floor conference room felt to Grey as though it was taken from a cheap action film: he could barely see past the dark wood round table, which was only illuminated by a handful of gold table lamps, fitted with a cheap green plastic lampshade that reminded him of the pub he had sat in earlier. The wide north-west window blinds were shut; nonetheless, some rogue yellow rays of sun managed to penetrate the otherwise poorly lit room.

The building's official name was the SIS Building at Vauxhall Cross, but was referred to as Babylon-on-Thames. Grey preferred the latter, as its architectural style looked like something inspired by the buildings of an ancient civilization.

It seemed to him like a messy cream coloured brick-made pile facing the muddy River Thames. Distinctively different in both shape and colour from anything else around, there was nothing like it anywhere in London. It was essentially comprised from three structures each higher than the other, with twin turrets erected in the top middle, uniting them. Between the turrets, dead at the centre, was a rounded terrace that reminded Grey of a Roman shrine. The floors differed from one another in size and shape, but kept perfect symmetry on both east and west wings. Each structure was topped with glossy turquoise windows.

People affectionately nicknamed it Legoland, as it looked like something assembled in a rush. Symmetrical rush, but a rush nonetheless, Grey thought to himself as he lifted one of the shades and looked down at the building. As the window blind pulled up electronically, the room was washed with a yellow light from the descending sun. Opposite Grey, with his back to the door, sat Neil Finch. He was forty-five years old, with dark hair greying in a few silvery streaks, and was balding at the very top. He had a piercing gaze as he listened to the other attendants, but his tough rugged look was otherwise diminished by his slouching shoulders. He was wearing a white shirt with a black and grey striped tie that reflected neither authority nor much creativity.

Next to Finch sat Matt Wey, MI6 Internal Comptroller, referred to by a derogatory term 'SIS Grass' behind his back. He was a young man, in respect to the heavy responsibilities laid on his shoulders, only thirty-seven years in age. He had a blond crew-cut, he was tall and slender, with a pale white skin that would lean towards pink after just a day in the sun. He spoke in a deep Essex accent with a sense of self-importance, that could not be perceived as authoritative by anyone else but himself. He was considered very smart, a meteor lawyer who had risen in the ranks of the Foreign Office's legal department, 'parachuted' into this post at MI6 by the Permanent Under-Secretary himself. The fact that he was welcomed in some corridors of Whitehall and never actually saw any fieldwork, made Wey unpopular among the SIS servicemen, to say the least. He was branded by many who had never even bothered to get to know him, as an opportunist suck up, and he was quite used to roaming the SIS building on his own like a leper.

"You see..." Finch started, with his heavy Sheffield accent. "The guys that visited your informant this AM are from E Squadron."

He nodded in understanding. He expected nothing less. The E Squadron was the name given to a special-ops unit performing covert operations. They were sometimes referred to as 'the Increment' and were a relatively newly formed unit subordinated to SIS directly. It was formed so that MI6 wouldn't need to use Special Forces such as SAS or SBS that were legally under the authority of the Ministry of Defence. Only a handful of people in the service had the authority to sign off on an E Squadron directive. Moreover, the three men were quite aware of the fact that it would take the very top to authorize an activity on English soil.

"We have no way of knowing what they were doing and why. And when C's secretary brushed me off under false pretences, I decided to put Mr Wey here in the loop." He exhaled heavily as soon as he said it.

Dark clouds were forming in Grey's mind. C was the long lasting nickname of the head of MI6. The alias was named after Mansfield Cummings, who was the founder and first to head what was then called 'the Secret Service Bureau'. He used to sign every official paper with the letter, and thus every head of what later evolved to be MI6 kept the initial. If the head was involved, things may run deeper than what he suspected, and it might be that Ephraim was on to something. *Your service is rotten.* The words echoed in his head.

"If the boss is sweeping this under the rug," he continued, "then Mr Wey here's the only one that can look into it—"

"Exactly," Wey interrupted. His accent stood up in contrast to Finch's rugged deep tones. His nasal pronunciation made him sound condescending. "Since I am the Internal Comptroller, I will be using my budget to appoint you to investigate. I trust you will accept the nomination?"

Was he always so formal? Grey nodded.

"It will be an ad hoc appointment. Once we are happy that we've got to the bottom of this, HR will handle the paperwork. Until then, you are essentially…"

"A rogue," Grey completed the sentence.

"Well," Wey squirmed. "I mean… I don't want whoever is behind this to get the head's up that you are sniffing the grass. If E Squadron were employed, it means that whoever it is has a high enough clearance to have access to anything, possibly even some of my files. But he can't see something that isn't filed, now can he? Since most of your work – I'd assume – will be naturally in the field, there's no need to find you a nice cubicle here in Legoland."

"Naturally."

"I will however give you access to my clearance level and files—"

"I don't think that's a good idea," Finch interrupted.

Wey's eyebrows shot up, he was obviously not used to being overruled.

"With all due respect, sir, if it's a high up insider, maybe even C himself, then he may find a way to access your private logs as well. I'm sure Agent Grey is resourceful and wise enough to see things my way."

Agent Grey. It had been a while. Was he back on the inside? It certainly didn't feel like it. "In other words," Grey said, extrapolating, "Mr Finch here wants me to parachute behind enemy lines without as much as even a radio. That way, if I'm apprehended, he can deny any connection to me. Just a mad old goat." He smiled cynically.

"Spot on." Finch looked at him, exposing a smile full of crooked yellow teeth.

Grey was fond of the old mid-level officer. He remembered him when he still had a head full of dark hair. Most instructors in the Ranch, where Grey served in the last years of his career, branded Finch a technocrat, a grey minor details guy. He disagreed, and was glad to see that he had called it right.

"What's next?" Grey asked.

"Two things we know," Wey declared and stood up quickly in an exaggerated manner. "First, someone who has the authority to activate E Squadron is involved. There are only a handful of people that can match this description. Second, a query I ran found no recent records of Henry Haft, save the conversation Finch had with you. This tells us that whoever is behind this went to great lengths to cover his tracks."

"Well that's not much," Finch blurted. "It's not like whoever would be doing something dodgy would bother documenting it. Right?"

Grey went to the window and sunk into the black leathered chair. "It does tell us one thing." He leaned forward on the table crossing his arms. "Whoever sent the E Squadron goons is working relentlessly so that no one in the service learns about it. We have to let them think that they're safe, therefore the two of you are more than welcome to kick me out of here."

Finch nodded. It would take some acting on Wey's part, and he wondered if he had it in him.

"We meet again on Monday at 9 am. Here. If I don't make the meeting, I suggest you update the head, the head of MI5 as well and the Under-Secretary. I'm hoping that at least one of them isn't bent, if not the lot." He swallowed hard.

"Are we done? Am I to discredit you now?" Wey asked.

"Yessir." Grey stood up. "Let's step outside to the corridor so you can literally throw me down the stairs in a way that anyone who's currently in operations can see and tell."

At that exact moment Grey's mobile rang.

Their conversation was curt. Grey didn't appreciate the fact that John had no understanding of phone tapping and SIGINT surveillance. Didn't the guy watch any spy movie for fuck's sake? John had tried to describe his revelation to Grey but the latter stopped him short and shifted the conversation to some witness declaration he neglected to have him sign. The two scheduled to meet in an hour or so outside Sloane Square's Underground station.

***

Liz Shaw was standing in the corner, facing the greengrocer stand as John entered Liverpool Street's Underground station. Her instructions were clear. She went over them in her mind: track him down, follow him, and report any contact he may be meeting. The number she had to report back to was unknown to her. She was to use a different phone from her own – it had been delivered by the mailroom earlier in the day. No sender ID. Most unusual.

As he walked into the station, she had been holding open a round pocket mirror-case, pretending to check her red lipstick. She had large plump lips that had been often sought after by her male classmates as early as when she was in grammar school. She had received the nickname the 'Black Widow' not just because of her charcoal black hair: she normally accepted the boys' date requests, yet dumped them the very next week. The ivory tone of her face stood in perfect contrast to the shade of her hair. She had catlike green eyes and a sharp nose that held firm her big-frame glasses. She wore black leather trousers, black boots, and a baggy cream sweater that nearly reached her knees, topped with a cream coloured trench. She had a slender and athletic physique underneath, but was accustomed to baggy clothes while on surveillance, as there wasn't much point in drawing unwanted male attention when posing as a shadow. That was one of her old instructor's mantras, and it stuck. Generally she loved attention from men; she felt empowered whenever a bloke, who was walking with his partner, turned his head to her. Silly, simple creatures she thought them, maybe that's the reason she never settled down with a permanent partner.

Liz observed John as he passed the greengrocer, he picked up his pace and traversed the station. It was buzzing and it seemed as though every one of the twenty-odd electronic gates was being used. An African-accented guard was standing in the corner trying to explain something to a group of Spanish tourists. They did not understand him and were drawing near him in a semicircle; it looked like he was about to be devoured.

As John went past the automatic gate, she snapped the mirror shut and made her way after him. The doors of the white plastic worm-like train had already beeped when she jumped on board, keeping him in close proximity as the train left the station.

As the train was gaining speed, Liz tried to figure out what Ops could possibly want from the clueless cute lad. 'Ops' or 'Covert Ops' was the service's directorate of special operations. It covered activities such as tailing subjects, sting operations and practically any ground or preparation work that a handler needed in order to carry out his job. They were divided into teams that rotated, but when they were home in Britain, they were generally given solo missions or exercise drills in order to keep them sharp. She had joined the service right after uni and was assigned to Ops based on her good looks and physical abilities (she had been a gymnast in secondary school among other hobbies). She was trained in the arts of surveillance and was taught how to read people. Training was tedious; it went on for two years and included excruciating hours and hours of mock surveillance exercises, interrogations and interviews, and mastering the use of firearms and explosives. Just what every good girl needs to know. Her overall performance at 'the Ranch', the nickname for SIS School of Intelligence, had been superb. She was a natural. After she graduated, she was permanently stationed in the Ops UK team, an honour normally saved for the best. To date she had had two lengthy major missions abroad. Every operation she had ever been involved in went without a glitch and she had received numerous commendations.

Throughout the years the occasional surveillance mission became such a routine that she could do it with her eyes closed. She learned to lay low, limit the questions to a minimum and collect the pay cheque at the end of the month. That attitude made her a sought after commodity within Ops, and she was quite aware of it. The job was gratifying, and the numerous missions kept her interest, in spite of the fact that surveillance activity was a bore ninety per cent of the time. While she was perfectly content professionally, the long and irregular hours, the abrupt abroad assignments and the fact that she couldn't discuss her work with anyone, made dating almost impossible. Besides, the 'Black Widow' had long found Englishmen in their thirties, tedious and full of themselves: a stereotype that formed based on the professional crowd that she mixed with. As she turned thirty, her parents, who had been retired for a few years now in Kent, stopped pressuring her into marriage, and focused on her younger sister, who was already a mother to twin boys. They simply had given up on her.

With her head clouded with thoughts, she left the train at Sloane Square station tailing the young target, almost automatically. The station was dark and uninviting, and as she climbed up the stairs she caught a glimpse of him meeting up with a man near the newspapers and snacks kiosk that was situated to the right-hand side of the cobblestone square. The other man was meticulously dressed, his hair was greyish and he was tall. She couldn't shake the thought that something in the guy looked awfully familiar.

As she came near, she drew out her phone and took a quick snapshot of the duo. Ops had devices which were enhanced with a real camera shutter, so the picture was sharp and the features were distinctive even with a photo taken in a brisk movement. She kept walking past them, and stopped as she crossed the street, just in time to see the pair take a left turn to Lower Sloane Street. She input the picture to a MMS and sent it to the unfamiliar number that had sent her instructions.

She had started striding on their tail as a message was received. It read: 'Adam Grey. Former SIS. Keep monitoring'.

Adam Grey. The last time she had seen the charming old spymaster he was lecturing at her class. That was back at the Ranch, he was about eight years younger and his hair wasn't nearly as grey. Could time have flown by so quickly? He had quite the reputation of being the best in their field. She would have to take extra care.

***

The deceptive sun had risen her head through the clouds, yet hadn't generated any sort of heat to somewhat dissolve the cold air. The duo sat at a local Italian deli called La Bottega. The place was cosy. They took the outside bench pressed to the big shopfront window, the outdoor heater providing them with comfortable warmth. There were only a few people sitting inside by the big glass counter which was packed with pastas and salads. Liz had quickly gotten in and occupied the corner table; she could see their backs pressed against the bench from the big window. Not the prefect vista point but this would have to do. She ordered a glass of white wine and stayed put.

John ordered a cappuccino and Grey a double espresso with San Pellegrino. "Nothing else, thanks," Grey told the mousy-haired waitress impatiently.

"We'll discuss your phone security awareness on a different occasion." He was snappy, continuing a conversation they had started on the way. "Now, what have you got for me?"

John produced the brown Jiffy from the inner pocket of his coat. He laid it on the table just as the drinks arrived. Grey's gaze darted between the envelope, John and the waitress. Liz made a mental note of that.

As the waitress left them Grey eased up a bit. "What is it?"

"Something in his final words made me realize where this was. To make a long story short – I spotted it next to a portrait of the Queen."

"What's in it?" He found it hard to hide his excitement over the revelation, facing the relaunching of Ephraim's murder investigation. Murder. He was now certain of it.

"I don't know," he answered. "I didn't open it."

With a swift motion Grey put his hand on the Jiffy and tore it open. He took out its contents: two passports, some official documents written in a foreign language and a letter. He had enough experience to identify the documents as Polish. The passports were Polish as well, bearing the names 'Peter Piotrowski' and 'Lukas Kozik'. He immediately noticed that the pictures in each passport were identical: a sixty-year-old man, with an aquiline nose and a thick grey moustache. He was unshaven and had thin shoulder length grey hair. He was wearing old style framed glasses.

The documents contained the same names, but had no pictures. They were official Polish interior ministry declarations. He picked up the letter, which was scribbled with an untidy handwriting. It bore yesterday's date.

Dear Mr Murray,

I am writing you this letter since I fear that my life is under genuine threat. You will soon realize that there is real foundation for my concerns. My son, Petr Haft, has been working for five years now in the Polish Foreign Office in Warsaw. His main job is to authorize citizenship requests and visa applications that are sent back to Warsaw for deeper scrutiny.

Petr had an acquaintance in the London consulate and together they authorized a few requests unlawfully, in aim of making extra money. I have given him quite a go when I heard, but this is of no importance now. His friend would pass the requests officially, they had a local lawyer that translated documents and sent them necessary legal letters for a fee, and his friend would then issue the passports in London. Very untraceable.

It is a criminal behaviour that I condemn, but times in Warsaw are tough and in general their actions have never hurt anyone.

After handling the papers of the gentlemen enclosed in this envelope, Petr came to visit me in

Joni Dee

London. He had found his acquaintance in London – Jerzy – dead in his flat. You may have heard about it, the police branded it as suicide, but the guy's details were never released to the press, as it was a matter involving a foreign national diplomat. I can assure you that the guy loved partying and was quite the ladies' man, and that suicide, according to Petr, is out of the question.

Jerzy's flat was torn apart, according to the police by squatters, but in Petr's opinion they were trying to retrieve these documents that I have enclosed. They were mistaken to think that Jerzy was in possession of them.

Despite my old age and crumbling memory I am certain that if you run these documents through your computers you will find the pictures strike an amazing resemblance to Professor Vasiliy Nikolayev. We had run into him around 1986 if I am not mistaken.

If nothing else, your integrity was never in doubt with me, Murray. Two days ago Petr went into hiding, in a location that even I do not know. I implore you to find whoever is behind this and help Petr. I can only assume that if Professor Nikolayev resurfaced, the worst is yet to come. What happens to me is immaterial as long as you do what is right.

Sincerely yours,

Ephraim

A gentleman to the very end, Grey thought. He could sense John's curiosity burning inside of him. "Well, you had it within your grasp and you were honest enough to keep it unopened – you might as well…" he said as he gave the letter to John. He already decided he would trust him, and thought it was good for someone else to have this information in case something happened to him.

As the young man took his time with it, Grey couldn't help but feeling melancholic. Nikolayev was a Soviet nuclear scientist, of the worst kind. He was a colonel in the KGB, the head of their secret Nuclear Proliferation Program. For nearly a decade, aided by quality espionage techniques, he managed to advance the USSR's nuclear program by light years. As the Soviet Bloc fell, everyone was certain that he would assume the same role at SVR, the Russian intelligence service, but the guy disappeared, presumed dead. There were rumours of his involvement with the Pakistanis and later the North Koreans, but there was never any corroboration. He was identified dead by the Americans in 2001, though the circumstances of his presumed hit were not shared with the service.

He had also remembered Jerzy's case vaguely. A young Polish diplomat who ended his life with a single gunshot in his Camden flat after the diplomatic womanizer was exposed as secretly gay, by an ex-lover. He never gave any thought to this case before.

His task was quite clear to him now. Someone in the service was aiding the formerly deceased Professor Nikolayev, making efforts to help his resurrection stay clandestine. He needed to find out why and then track down Ephraim's son. He owed him that much. He studied his reflection in the shop's window: he suddenly seemed to look ten years older.

Chapter 5
Ephraim

He started running. Portland Place, a big and normally busy street, home to many of the foreign embassies present in the capital, now seemed abandoned. The freezing dewy London air penetrated his bones, yet beneath the woollen overcoat and sweater, his back was sweating.

An ambulance's siren was heard in the distance. Yes. Definitely an ambulance, they differ from the police sirens that are whaling up and down. Too bad, if it was a police car he would have run towards the source of the sound for protection. Soon he will pass by the luxurious Langham Hotel, then a few more steps and he will be safe among the stream of tourists walking up and down Oxford Street. Sunday afternoon, there are bound to be tourists there, he convinced himself, even though London was rather dreary and empty these days. He kept his pace, taking off his wide rim fedora that amidst the run caused his scalp to itch.

From Oxford Street he will find a phone box and call Murray. Murray was a good lad, too young but serious enough to actually know his way around. His old handler

And the Wolf Shall Dwell

Wilshere had retired, so he was told, but he knew the truth: the body found last week in Regent's Park was surely his. He read about it in the newspaper, a balding male in a tweed suit, same height, same build and same age as Wilshere. There were no signs of violence and nothing was taken. His curiosity had sent him to Regent's Park the following day; he had spotted traces of expensive Italian shoes in the mud near the spot where the body was discovered. Who walks around the mud with shoes like that? The thought that the British service men can't even defend themselves in their own backyard gave him the chills.

He had arrived at Oxford Street already out of breath, exhaling cold vapour and sweating all over. He had switched to a rapid walk. The feeling of terror had slid down his throat and hit him in the gut, but so did the awareness that he simply had to complete his mission. For his country's sake. A red double-decker passed him from the right-hand side, and as it slowed down a few people jumped off without waiting for the bus to pull into its station. The British efforts to take Poland out of the Warsaw Pact had gone sour. The British government is so vain, he thought to himself. What did they expect? On one hand they keep supporting the exiled government that does as little as distributing propaganda from their base on Eaton Street, while on the other hand they are conducting talks with the communists. It suits the Brits to try and hold the stick from both ends, and then to approach little old Henry to try and figure out where they stand. His mood seemed better under the protection of the Oxford Street shoppers. He coughed. He had entered the first phone box that he came across his way, near Bond Street, and rang Murray's number.

Two hours later, as the twilight dissolved and gave way to the early December evening, he sat on a bench in the north end of Hyde Park, close to Speakers' Corner. It was way too late for speeches held by eccentric individuals that took place on that spot during the hours of the day. He was practically alone in the park. His features were indistinguishable, protected by the nightly shadows that defeated the faint lamp post light. In the future, from this placid spot, one would be able to hear the commotion of the winter amusement park 'Winter Wonderland'. Today, since the sun set so lazily early, even the remote traffic of the otherwise busy Marble Arch roundabout seemed muted, as if it was the dead of the night rather than the early evening hours.

A sound of boots grinding the wet leaves was heard from the cement path. Earlier, he made sure to meticulously mark the tree to the right of the bench with a distinctive white chalk stripe, a prearranged signal suggesting that he hadn't been followed. The fact that two figures emerged into the pale orange light worried him. It was not what they agreed upon over the phone, he thought.

Both silhouettes wore light mackintoshes, completely inappropriate for the freezing temperatures. As they approached he noticed that they were both wearing old fashioned bowler hats that were much more common a decade or more earlier. As they came near, the street light revealed two faces. English. The younger man of the two casually addressed him by saying, "It's already snowing in Warsaw."

They were waiting for him to complete the sentence for reassurance that this is indeed their guy and that everything was in order, yet he kept silent. He thought he recognized Murray's voice, but he wasn't sure. Besides, he decided he wanted to see how the men would react when facing uncertainty. As the seconds passed, he could clearly see that the other fellow was reaching to an object concealed from sight under his mackintosh. A gun?

"So far here in London it's only cold," he finally blurted out the other half of the code, and could immediately see the men's faces become a lot less tense.

They both stepped closer to the bench. The other guy, who he presumed wasn't Murray, took out a cigarette and lit it without even as much as offering one. Rude, he thought.

"This wasn't what we agreed," Ephraim finally said. "I could have easily given you guys the slip, seeing you both down the path."

"Relax," Grey tried to reassure him. "Jamie here is a colleague, he can be trusted."

Grey's face was clean shaven, and without a hint of a wrinkle on it. The second man was named Jamie Jensen, he was an Operations Room Executive Officer, recruited by the service only a year or so before Grey. He had a rugged look, with a high forehead and a receding front hairline, which made his forehead seem even larger. The addition of narrow eyes and stringy eyebrows gave his face a clownish appearance. He was smoking his Woodbine brand cigarette slowly, and kept glancing at anyone who passed by. Jensen was never a handler, that's why they didn't even bother coming up with an alias for him. He was there as a favour to Grey. The incident involving agent Wilshere who was murdered in Regent's Park called for a new protocol within the service, in relation to meeting up with sources or agents. Handlers were to request a security team for every meeting, and authorization was to be sought in advance.

Since Ephraim's call came in so suddenly, and Grey had never actually met him, he decided to accommodate him and agreed to meet on the day. If Ephraim wants to dance – let's dance, he had thought to himself. He didn't want this lead to go cold. Since no security team was to be obtained so promptly, the alternative was to simply ask Jamie, who was the executive operations officer in charge, to accompany him to the meeting at the end of his shift. This was highly unorthodox, but at least he wasn't going alone. So far, Grey thought, Jamie was on form. He was holding his Walther PPK covertly, and he appeared to be tightening the grip whenever a stranger was drawing near them.

Another minute of silence had passed between them. Grey didn't push any questions. He knew better than to put a source on the spot. He will eventually talk, he thought to himself, they always did.

A lone cyclist passed by. When the sound of the bicycle wheels ticking on the path's concrete subsided, Ephraim started talking again. "They are using us, Murray." His voice was trembling. "The Russians. They are using us to enhance their nuclear arsenal." Grey kept his silence.

"I found documents from the Warsaw Pact. I don't normally have access to them, but a couple of weeks ago the guy that used to do it got called back to Poland, so I've been filing these for his department."

"Which department is that?"

"*Ministerstwo Obrony Narodowej.*" The Polish Ministry of National Defence, he said the name in Polish. "I brought them with me, but I need to return them as soon as possible."

Grey was overwhelmed. It wasn't Ephraim's statement regarding the Eastern Bloc's nuclear proliferation that shook him. Grey saw these reports himself. It was the fact that Ephraim had such complete access to the Ministry's correspondence. Ephraim was clearly the kind of source that could build careers and Grey imagined just how far he could go.

"So you said you have the documents with you?"

"Yes."

"Were you made?"

"Excuse me?"

"Did they spot you taking these documents with you? You sounded hysterical when we talked."

"I can't say. Leaving the embassy I thought two security guys followed me and I panicked. Either I lost them in the West End, or it was my nerves playing tricks on me, like you English say. I haven't noticed anything since, so I went ahead with the meeting."

"Okay," Grey answered. "We can't waste any more time…" He took out a tiny silver pocket camera. "This is a state of the art espionage camera. We will equip you with one once we know you haven't been made, so that you needn't take risks like that again. Now let's hope that the light here will be enough for us."

Ephraim nodded as Grey approached him. Jamie Jensen scrutinized the pair with penetrating dark eyes. He drew a lengthy pull from his cigarette and threw the butt into the darkness.

Joni Dee

Chapter 6
Babylon-on-Thames: Present Day

He sat on an indulgent office chair by a heavy chestnut desk inside an office located on the eighth floor of the Babylonian-like building. For a couple of hours now the sun had shone without any interrupting clouds, and the thick glass window overlooking the Thames had made a greenhouse-effect, which heated his back. It felt nice.

Below the window was a cabinet that matched the colour of the desk, it had a silver framed picture of his family on it – a good looking blonde woman in her fifties and two teenage girls with strawberry-blonde-coloured hair, dressed in matching sailing kits. The desk housed a PC screen, a mouse and a keyboard, a digital phone with a touch screen and a silver ashtray. On the wall to the right was a chestnut coloured bookcase, with few books and a model of the Russian ABM-4, Anti-Ballistic Missiles Launcher, the Gorgon.

He double clicked Internet Explorer but before typing in the username and password in the Gmail login page, he launched a program from the task bar which would encrypt what he would now work on, even from his own IT department. In fact, without a password that only C possessed today, no one could even check his browsing history. That will prevent the snoops from IT checking up on him in one of their useless routine keyword searches. He chuckled to himself, well aware that he was one of the Counter Intelligence Committee members that came up with this protocol.

The exemption from complete scrutiny was granted as part of the Chinese walls policy that the service had undertaken a few years back. The beneficiaries of this privilege were the then-active department heads and above. At the time, an overriding password was given to C, to a few senior department heads and to the vice chief. These department heads were long retired, and with the idiot vice chief forced to resign a month ago over a sex scandal that went public, well… de facto the only man who could expose him was C himself.

If it wasn't for his relatively old age he would have been the natural candidate to be the new vice chief. But because he was closing on the big six-o, he knew he had already reached his glass ceiling. He sometimes wondered how he managed to last as head of the Counter Intelligence Department for so long.

It took him a while to secure the position. His department was a small one as counter intelligence was mainly dealt with by the MI5. But still he had numerous resources, and his word carried a heavy weight among the other department heads.

He punched in username and his password 'WoodB123'. He found one single message in his inbox:

From: Lazarus

Received: 2:02 am

My Dearest Martha,

I hope you are well.

The documents you were meant to help me obtain did not reach their destination!

I hope the bearer's demise was not premature.

Do you need me to send someone to help you handle the matter?

Please reach out asap.

    Yours,

    Lazarus

He moaned. Always a dash of drama. Lazarus was never fond of delays. He had read the memos regarding Henry Haft's death. But without actually retrieving the documents, there was no telling if the old man actually had them or the apes from the Increment simply decided to push an innocent man to his death. His role as head of the Counter Intelligence Department in this case would play as a double-edged sword. From one side he could find it easy to cover up his tracks if things went sour; on the other hand, it would be easily uncovered that he gave direct instructions to the Ops teams.

His phone vibrated. He picked it up. It was a picture of Adam Grey. He rolled his eyes. Only Grey can come back from the abyss and ruin his plans. He remembered seeing Grey earlier in the day, but he took no notice of him at the time. He decided that once he finished replying to bloody

Lazarus, he would open the secure bulletin board and check any mentioning of Haft. If Ephraim was involved somehow with Lazarus' documents, someone would have blurted it by now.

To: Lazarus

From: Jrj2000@gmail.com

You have nothing to fear. I have already initiated the process of issuing you alternative documents from a different shop, which I will deliver to you personally.

The originals will be retrieved and happiness will roam our household once again.

Martha

He smiled. Lazarus would appreciate the lyric touch. He added the words *'Yours truly'* and clicked on the envelope icon to send the message. He closed the encryption software and hit a key on his desk phone.

"Yes, sir," a female voice came through.

"Helen, send me anything that went through the Thoth system in the last couple of days with the tags Ephraim, Henry, Haft, Poland and…" He hesitated. "Adam Grey. That'll be all."

"Yes, sir, I'll send it over immediately."

He hung up. His phone vibrated again. It was Liz Shaw, the message was simple, and it read 'they are in possession of an envelope. Cannot retrieve without making contact. Engage?'

He put the phone down on the desk. Good job, Agent Shaw, he thought to himself, but this will be a far more elaborate job than you could handle. In spite of Grey's advanced age, he was still one of the best they had. Plus, he didn't want Shaw to accidentally read the material in hand.

He went back to the computer and opened the service inner mail system and punched in a simple work order:

To: E Admin, E Group, Ops – all
CC: C

Targets have been identified by Agent Shaw. Picture to follow.
Objective: retrieval of documents in their possession.
Means: any.
Authorization code J-1-5-0-7-8-1
  Execute immediately.

He picked up the phone and forwarded Grey and the guy's picture to his secretary. He added a caption that read 'attach to my last sent email, as a new msg. same recipients except C'. It is far too early for C to be made aware that one of ours is involved.

He hesitated then sent the message. He picked up his phone and replied to Agent Shaw's text. 'Negative. Keep monitoring and report any change in circumstances'. He sent the message. He opened his desk drawer. It contained a diary, a Walther PPK and a pack of nicotine chewing gum. He took out two gum pellets and leaned back in his chair.

Chapter 7
Chelsea

Liz was monitoring Grey and the guy closely. They were still seated at the wooden table engaged in their conversation, when the sun had disappeared without a warning behind the grey clouds. She had noticed movement on the upper part of the street. Black Range Rovers were piling up, and the people passing by on Lower Sloane Street seemed, for a fraction of a second, frozen in time.

Grey got up abruptly, and with a sharp movement flipped the wooden table on its side. The guy jumped up an instant after, in what appeared to Liz like an alley cat's instinct of self-preservation. It was quite apparent that he had no prior training. Who was this guy?

The two exchanged some inaudible words, then immediately thrusted into a frantic run down the street. One of the Range Rovers managed to get past a bus that was blocking the two-way traffic. It drove onto the pavement near the deli and pulled up in front of an old phone box that was blocking its passage. Three agents exited from the vehicle, guns in hand, amid cries from panicking bystanders.

E-Squadron apes, Liz thought to herself, while she started walking inconspicuously closer to the scene. Ops would have been so much more subtle and discrete, which would have resulted with the pair already apprehended. She sighed.

As they were running, Grey caught a glimpse of the abandoned Range Rover parked on the pavement and the agents running in pursuit. Luckily for them, the traffic on Chelsea Bridge was heavy, which caused the entire street to be congested; the other vehicles were held back and could not join the chase.

Grey deduced that no more agents would engage on foot, as they were already too far behind. They would instead likely try to block them from the south bank. He already decided to avoid crossing the bridge – they would stand better chances taking on the remaining three. On his signal, they crossed the street running, an act immediately copied by the pursuing agents.

"ADAM GREY, HALT!" a shout was heard from behind. The cry pumped up the adrenaline levels in his body like a burst of caffeine. It had kept him sharp and on point, making him analyse every possible route of escape. He was very much aware now of the Jiffy envelope which was sitting heavily in his suit pocket.

"Keep running!" he yelled to John, who was starting to fall behind. Led by Grey, they had picked up their pace, running on the bicycle lane of the Chelsea Bridge Road. To their right stretched the fence of Ranelagh Gardens park. John's breathing grew heavy, and Grey knew he needed to give him a break or else… He slowed down and turned, stooping into a crouching position. The three pursuing agents immediately took cover and ducked behind the parking cars. It was a risky move given the fact that Grey had no gun, but it paid off. The gesture was enough to give him an edge over their pursuers, and as he caught up with John, the E Squadron agents were just picking themselves up from their positions.

John felt the rush of adrenaline enhancing his senses too. He felt like he was in an action film. It was absurd. As they were closing on the bridge, they started slowing down and John turned to Grey, desperate for air – all too conscious of a burning sensation in his lungs.

"Grey! What the hell? Shouldn't we just turn ourselves—" a whistling thump cut him short. It sounded like a gunshot but he couldn't be sure. The agents were still far from sight. With a brisk movement Grey grabbed to the top of the garden's fence and lifted himself over it but his ankle got stuck, and scratched in the process. Within a millisecond he managed to push himself over the fence with the other leg and leap, then landed on the other side. John followed the move and managed to do it swiftly and flawlessly. They then started making their way inside the foliage at the rim of the park, Grey limping.

Was that a real gun shot? They kept walking in the high shrubbery, hearing their pursuers reach the embankment, then trying to decide whether to walk up the bridge or to look elsewhere.

They continued advancing quietly in the foliage, and soon they could see a glimpse of the big brick building of the Royal Hospital from their hiding place, despite its low height. Grey knew that the former hospital was now a retirement home for old army veterans. They would need to keep quiet in order to blend in, this was no place to run into with a bleeding leg or the authorities will be made aware of their presence.

They kept crouching low, checking their surroundings. They couldn't hear any further chasing sounds. In fact they could hear no sounds at all save their heavy breathing. The impeccably groomed lawn area was empty, and none of the army veterans who had normally roamed the premises were visible. Grey pointed to the main building and gave a snappy hand signal, he would feel a lot safer in the inner courtyard. They initiated in a low crouch-run from the treeline to the main hall, which subsided to a slower nervous walk when they reached the front iron fence. Grey kept signalling John to walk slowly in a calmer manner, so they would not be as noticeable from a distance. As Grey pointed, they kept striding on the dirt path and kept off the grass, trying to pass as staff or visitors. However, it was quite apparent that they didn't belong.

Grey's leg was bleeding heavily now, and his trousers were drenched. "Why don't we just talk to them and figure it out?" John broke the silence. "You can tell them that I have nothing to do with all this, and let me get on with my life." Grey walked a few paces before he finally stopped, he let a whole minute run its course before he answered.

"You do realize they fired at us, right?" He was trying to shock him. "I'm afraid, Mr Daniel, that you've made yourself very much involved in this. If nothing else, blame Henry for making you a part of it when he gave you the key to finding these documents." He patted his pocket to make sure that the envelope was still in its place.

They started walking again and kept their pace. John was frowning as he walked.

"Walk regularly," Grey commanded. "They may very well be watching, though I think we lost them."

"Who are they?"

"They're Special Unit guys, I think some Special Ops unit, possibly the Increment."

"Increment? Special Ops?" John sounded confused.

"They must have followed you – that's how they knew where we were. We will have to work on your secretive conduct, or lack of one." He was testing John's patience. He would need him more focused if he had no choice but to keep the kid with him until this was resolved.

"You're bleeding." John pointed at Grey's leg.

"We will also need to work on your attention to details; I nearly lost a pint already."

Baiting him seemed to have worked, as John now seemed genuinely annoyed. Grey's gaze kept trailing between the different surroundings: the treeline; the building's wide roof; the old ceremonial cannons situated behind them. He was assessing anything that may look out of place.

They reached the cobblestone path and crept into the main hall. It was empty. The old veteran house was as deserted as an old minefield. It felt eerie. The black and white checked floor was shiny, reflecting the bright day which was still apparent through the windows. They could make out the fresco of the dark chapel room in the distance, a place where most of the lights were out. As they advanced into the chapel, Grey was looking for a back door or a way to exit north, towards Chelsea.

John was restless, he tried again getting Grey's attention, but the older man was driven and wouldn't halt. Grey had finally found a pathway leading to an exit door; he was trying to get it to open.

The wind whistled through the chapel, causing the wooden windows to bang against their frame. The big gust had put out the prayer candles, some were still smoking.

"ADAM!" John cried. The roar echoed throughout the chapel. Grey stopped fiddling with the door and turned around. He gave John a piercing look.

"I don't want any part in this!"

He was mad now, Grey thought. That was good. He couldn't make him sharper or physically stronger in a day, but at least he wasn't apathetic. He could work with mad.

"That, I'm afraid, is not up to me," he answered calmly and walked through the doorway.

***

The taxi was soaring on the road. "Do me a favour, mate, stay clear of the Chelsea Bridge please," Grey instructed the driver who acknowledged with a grunt.

He took out his phone and changed the SIM card with one that he fished out of a small nylon bag found in his pocket. He dialled a number.

"Finch, it's me."

John couldn't hear the man on the other end of the line. He saw the fatigue now apparent on the older man's face. His sweaty body odour had filled the taxi's interior. It wasn't just sweat. It was a mélange of sweat, blood and fear.

"Yes in broad daylight…"

Grey was recounting their near miss to the guy on the other end of the line, he was being extra cautious and selected his words meticulously, John noticed. Meanwhile the familiar Chelsea scenery was seen through the taxi's windows. After every few rich buildings they had passed, whether they were white with red bricks or simply white painted, came along an ugly council estate. These estates wore the all too familiar yellow creamy bricks and depressing brutalist architecture. The private parks in between were green and barricaded. All of a sudden he was aware that in the blink of an eye he had grown weary of this city. He sighed.

"The old place in Greenwich Village," Grey continued. "No! Don't type it in the computer in case they're monitoring your station—"

...

"—Yes of course I remember – King George Street, corner of Crooms Hill, by Greenwich Park. If we can't walk in, we'll be waiting at St Christopher Inn—"

...

"Yes, the old hotel by the train station. But try the flat first. There was an old lady not far off that used to keep the keys…"

The taxi cruised over Waterloo Bridge. John caught a glimpse of the blue-grey Thames water. It seemed like dark wrinkled satin in the faint glow of the setting sun. John remembered a picture by Monet, which portrayed the Thames behind Charing Cross Bridge, in it a sole dinghy. It was painted with bright light blue pastel colours. Traversing the Thames now, he wondered where the French artist managed to see such vivid shades in the drab river. He didn't see the resemblance to the river they had just passed, but he had to admit that it was a beautiful picture. He came back to reality when Grey's monotone chatter had been broken. "—and Finch, bring a first aid kit and a pair of size thirty-four trousers, will you?"

Joni Dee

Chapter 8
Sammy

The twilight had already fallen on Les Deus Margot café, in the Parisian neighbourhood of Saint-Germain-des-Prés. It was raining heavily and the white fabric of the outdoors wooden chairs was getting drenched. The few people that were sitting outside either took their coffees and ran indoors or simply abandoned the place. The inside was uncharacteristically gloomy. There were more dark crimson sofas left unoccupied than there were people. The black and white checked floor, hardly visible on most days due to vast waiters' movement, was left naked and exposed.

A clinking sound of two cups was highly audible, and an elderly woman in the back managed to drop her plate and to cause a chiming racket. The ringtone of a mobile phone pierced the air. A man poked in his grey trench coat pocket and retrieved an outdated Blackberry device. He was a dark Levantine, who was about sixty years old, his face was wrinkly from too much sun exposure and his erratic hair was white as snow. He had a cup of finished café noisette on the table, a copy of *Le Figaro*, an empty glass and a bottle of Perrier.

Everyone who was left in the café was staring at him, but he didn't seem to mind. "Go ahead," he said into his mobile, without even acknowledging that other people where around him. A woman who was sipping tea from an oversized mug was shaking her head as if this was otherwise a library.

"Sammy." An accented man was on the other end of the line.

"Yeah."

"We need you across the Channel. I took the liberty of booking you on the eight o'clock Eurostar."

"That's very soon." He was still calm and focused.

"Yeah."

"Care to elaborate?"

"There's a fuck-up."

"I'm not going to be detained at St Pancras? Just so they can dick me around again?"

"He assured me they will let you in this time."

"Accommodation?"

"The usual. Near the embassy in Kensington."

"Anything else?"

"No."

"Then I'd better get going." He nearly rang off.

"Samuel."

"Huh?"

"Offer the English your help, the station chief'll brief you. There's a lot at stake if this goes south."

He closed the phone. He dug in his trench's pocket and produced a ten euro note, which he left on the table. He hurried to the door, delaying to pick up a matching grey wide brim hat that was hanging on a hook. He put it on, walking out into the rain.

Chapter 9
A Safe House in Greenwich

"Overnight, you became one of the most wanted people in the realm, Mr Daniel," Neil Finch said humorously as he was pouring a glass of sparkling water taken from a small fridge in the stuffy bedroom.

John was sitting on the edge of the wide bed, the room was old and the décor seemed like it hadn't been replaced since the eighties. It had a revolting green floral wallpaper, and a beige fuzzy wall to wall carpet that smelled old and musty.

"Aren't you afraid to drink that? It's been here for more than a decade," Grey commented. He was sitting on a straw chair by a small wooden vanity table that had seen better days, and was dressing his ankle with a bandage.

"It's fine, water doesn't go bad." He grinned as he finished pouring the rest of the flat liquid.

"Have we learned anything new?" Grey asked. He was wearing khaki coloured trousers that Finch had brought him. They didn't really match his attire but they had to do, given that his suit trousers had a huge hole embellished with caked blood.

"The Americans are adamant that Nikolayev is dead." He had texted him the name when they were still in the cab.

"Why would Haft Junior set up a fake passport for a dead man?" Grey asked.

"I agree—" Finch responded apologetically but was cut off by Matt Wey who stormed into the room.

"The obvious answer is that he isn't," Wey said.

"And Haft?"

"An error on their part. The link is remote. They surely never imagined this will end up in the hands of a former serviceman."

"Jerzy?"

"Collateral damage. Could be that they meant to do with him in any event, tie loose ends. Haft's son too."

"And the E Squadron?" Finch asked.

"I've checked, and there are currently four people who could activate E Squadron without clearing it with C. That's disregarding C himself."

"We have to assume that any one of them or all of them combined can be involved then, and let's hope we're wrong about it!" Finch exclaimed.

"Can we not check their computers' history?" Grey was on edge.

"Well… Without an active vice chief, we have few people that are entitled to encryption, meaning we cannot check their activities if they choose to hide it, without C's password overriding it… Chinese walls… So I fail to see what good will it do to—"

"Can you check who pulled the trigger on the E Squadron? By activation of the authorization code maybe?" Grey suggested.

"Impossible. Authorization codes are punched into an automated encrypted system, I doubt anyone can access this."

"So what's next?" Finch asked.

"We need to rattle the cages and ferret them out. If something's amiss, whoever's responsible, C or one of the senior department heads, is bound to panic and make a mistake – provided we raise enough havoc." Finch stood up, his fist was clenched.

"The situation is quite clear to all of us, gents," Wey said, drawing attention to John with his finger. He was sitting in the same spot, staring into thin air in a state of shock. He became quite aware that all the eyes in the room were suddenly on him. He stood up and addressed no one in particular. "I hope you all realize that my part in this little adventure of yours is finished."

Nobody replied.

He then turned to Grey. "What else could you possibly want from me, Mr Grey? I provided you with THE lead, I was shot at… I'm done. Get me out of this mess. Go to the police and have them protect me if you must… Oh… Wait a second…" He was gaining momentum. "I almost forgot; you guys are the BLOODY POLICE or whatever it is you are, and according to the last ten minutes of babbling it's your own guys that are trying to kill us." He exhaled. The three had an astonished look on their faces, as if the rug was just pulled from beneath their feet. "So I'll ask you this once only – who's giving me a ride home or are you calling me a cab?"

There was a moment of silence and Grey stepped in. "You're a target as much as I am, John, I'm afraid you can't just walk away. We, I, still need your help."

"How fucking convenient." He lowered his voice. It looked like he was reflecting on what was said. "This is great. You are playing a John le Carré book, and I'm about to get it." He looked from one face to another, they were all expressionless. Emotionless. "What do you need from me?" he said placidly. "What's the end game?"

"Once we have enough evidence to link someone to these fake passports for this Russian scientist Nikolayev," Grey's voice was fatherly, he continued slowly, "we can take it to the Under-Secretary or the Attorney General. Then you'll be safe."

"Can you get me to your main computer?" John asked.

"It's not that easy!" Finch protested.

"Getting me physically there or logging in with an administrator password?" John was wondering what Finch was referring to.

"Bloody both!" he shouted.

"You are some sort of a computer genius, right?" Grey eyed John.

"I wouldn't say genius. I know my way around, and I did my thesis on algorithms and code break—"

"That'll have to do," Wey interrupted.

"That's pretty impressive," Grey shot Wey a rebuking glance.

"If I succeed; what then?" John said in a calm voice.

"We will seek justice," Wey assured him.

"Would I be left alone?"

"Yes," they both answered simultaneously.

"Then what are we waiting for?!" He jumped to his feet. "I'll need my laptop, otherwise there's a program I'll need to download, and the connection would be traced back to my company's servers, which I think is best to avoid."

Nobody flinched.

"Let's go!" John exclaimed.

"Patience, lad!" It was Finch. "We can't just barge in to the office in broad daylight and perform an act of sabotage. The picture of you two is all over the plasmas in Operations." He chuckled, but Grey and John's stares were grim.

"Don't worry," Grey said. "We'll book into a hotel tonight. We'll drop over at your flat and if the coast is clear, we'll get your laptop."

Finch shot him a bewildered look.

"I'm aware of the risk!" Grey shot back at him. "But I don't want to implicate his company and put his employment in jeopardy too, unnecessarily. We owe him this much," he said more calmly.

John turned to the window. The dusk started to set down on Greenwich's green hill and the Observatory. The few people out were slowly dispersing as the street lights seemed to be kicking in. A sombre feeling lay heavily upon him; he slowly came to realize that he was in way over his head.

Joni Dee

Chapter 10
Whitehall

A grey shadow engulfed the crimson coloured waiting hall leading to the office of the British Secretary of State for Defence. The mahogany bookcase was packed with hundreds of faint coloured and old books. A musty smell was hanging heavy in the air. The head of the service, Anthony Stamper, aka C, was sitting on a haggard green suede chair at the corner of the room. The heart of the highest authority in the British Intelligence Service was pounding fast and his face was pale.

Stamper, who used every opportunity he got to clink metal with the brass in Westminster, had tried to avoid this meeting by any means possible. It was a phone call from the Secretary himself that precluded him from skipping the meeting. The high ranking cabinet member made it clear to Stamper, who had already seen off three governments and four different secretaries, that this was a summoning and not a social call that could be evaded at his leisure. He felt a slight irritation in his throat, accompanied by a light choking sensation. He was sure that the relatively newly appointed

Minister wouldn't dare sack him so early in his term, but he was certainly not looking forward to the cold shower that he was about to get.

While he was waiting, his mobile phone vibrated.

"Stamper."

"They know," a cold voice was heard at the other end of the line.

"I know they know; you bloody fool." He contained his temper and didn't raise his voice that was already high enough to echo in the small entry hall. "How you managed a cock-up of such a scale for a simple thing like a passport is beyond me," he said quietly.

"What do you want me to do next then?"

"Start by calling off the Increment! Have you lost your fucking mind?" he snapped. He immediately regained his composure. "Use Ops only—"

"But—" the voice tried to protest.

"Do you have any idea where I am now?"

"Yes," he muttered.

"Then you understand that I am about to get a pile of shit dumped on my head for the mess you got us into."

"Right…"

"And unless you want this to come back at you, I suggest you figure it out. Are we clear?"

"Crystal."

"I have to go in now." The door was opening and a crack of dim light was spreading on the burgundy coloured carpet. "Keep me posted." He rung off exactly as the door came ajar. Beneath the crossbar stood Oliver 'Olly' Jones, the PM's advisor for state and foreign affairs. He was thirty-eight years young, with a full head of dark hair and a strong jawline. His vigorous appearance stood in contrast to Stamper's bald head and meagre physique.

Olly always seemed to Stamper as someone who had gotten way too much credit from the PM, who had only just managed to secure a second term in the general election held the previous year. Olly was a Cambridge and Insead graduate, and held the 'Position of Trust' with the PM ever since he was the Secretary of State for Energy and Climate Change. In his last Secretarial position before he took over the Conservative party, the PM was briefly the Secretary of State for Defence after a reshuffle ordered by his predecessor. During that period, young Olly was appointed to numerous key positions within the Joint Intelligence Committee and managed to get familiarized with the armed forces and military intelligence community. The presence of the PM's advisor rather than the Secretary himself made Stamper even more edgy.

The Tories were the ruling party for the past four consecutive terms, a fact that had facilitated life for Stamper as the head of the service. He didn't have to cope with any righteous left wing pansies that made his predecessor's life a living hell and crippled the service significantly. On the other hand, the last elections were won by a thread, and a coalition government had to be formed with the Lib Dems. This had made the PM profoundly weak. Stamper understood all too well that his golden era was up, and that any blown covert operation could immediately escalate into a scandal that could bring down the coalition.

"Come in, sir," Jones called. "I am sure you haven't got too much time for me, now have you?" He smiled. This smile made Stamper's blood freeze in his veins. The fact that Olly didn't bother to shake his held-out hand infuriated him.

"I was expecting Willow," he said as he dropped his leather designer valise on one of the green suede chairs inside the chamber. Willow, Sir Richard Willoughby, was the Secretary of State for Defence. He was an old shrewd fox who had been roaming the corridors of power with the Conservative party for a few decades now. Known to all as Sir Willow, Willoughby was always holding some unofficial position within the party, while secretly pulling the strings. However, he was asked by the PM to serve as a State Minister this time around, in an effort to keep the backbenchers in his party in line, for the sake of the fragile coalition.

"We decided it's better that I chat with you alone, before this thing gets out of hand." A young and attractive assistant stepped into the chamber and asked if they wanted coffee or tea. Before Stamper could answer, Olly Jones dismissed her. Stamper had been dying for a coffee since he arrived at Whitehall. It's bad enough that this impertinent pup made him wait, now he was being bluntly rude. He was making a point, very unsubtly.

Stamper was frowning, and he was well aware of it. It was hard not giving Jones the satisfaction. "What is it, Olly?" he snapped. "You said so yourself – I'm a busy man," he blurted as soon as the door closed behind the young high-heeled assistant.

"I, actually, he... actually, we would like to know if you're in control of the situation, Tony." He returned the favour by calling him in his shortened name, which he knew he hated. "We can't afford one of your underlings to bark up the wrong tree and expose our involvement."

"It's all under control. I left it with my men, I myself am in a position to deny involvement if it comes to this—"

"This is no longer an option."

"I beg your pardon?" He was enraged by Olly's boldness.

"And so you should!" The bite was unsubtle but Olly didn't care. "Both the PM and Sir Willow think that this thing has outgrown your underling. If the guy can't deliver, we expect you to handle the situation yourself. Roll up your sleeves for once, Tony, step into the mud."

Stamper was red with fury, it was bad enough that they had sent the errand boy to give him a shake-up, now it was turning into a dig – with him on the receiving end. "Listen, Olly," he was past politeness now. "You and your American friends wanted support from us. You didn't expect me to make this a service vision guideline now did you? I've just recently learned that a good officer, an old handler, has found a lead – you are aware that I cannot torpedo his investigation without having the JIC start making inquiries, right? Do you want to deal with a parliamentary investigation committee afterwards? Take a chill pill, and I suggest you give one to old Willow and the PM, and let us do our work."

Olly remained silent.

"Meanwhile, let's not lose our heads, and remember that I have a whole organization to run, and that the Iranian nuclear threat is just the tip of the iceberg. At the moment there are more than two hundred warnings for potential terrorist acts in Central London alone. Do you have any idea how many things are currently on my plate?"

"Fine, Stamper, you made your point. Just one thing, let's make it clear – if you can't control your boys and somehow word gets out—"

"It won't!"

"But if it does," Olly insisted, "I want you to know in advance that the PM will be genuinely surprised and will require that the bad apples in his intelligence services pay the maximum—"

"Don't threaten me, Olly. I know exactly what's at stake and if I fall, be sure that the Conservatives will fall down with me, even if you manage to somehow save the skin of the very top man in the pyramid." His words were directed at Olly himself. It was a fair assumption that if this ploy gets out, the PM will claim ignorance but the coalition will fall nonetheless.

"I won't pass your words to the PM, as a personal favour to you, Stamper. Just do what you signed up for and let us worry about steering the foreign policy and global public view. And make sure no rogue agents mess this up for us."

"Our interests are the same here. Tell that to the PM."

"One more thing. The Israelis offered their help."

"Do our friends in Langley know?"

"They said it was up to us whether to accept."

"Interesting… Any idea who they sent?"

"Sammy. Does the name ring a bell?"

"That vulture is now welcomed again to English soil?"

"Nah, the Israeli Minister for Intelligence and Strategic Matters said he can get here quickly. We had to sort his arrival with the Border Police. Mossad is quite eager to get this Nikolayev business public before the American Secretary of State arrives in the Middle East next month. They all agree that if we wait till the last minute, things can get catastrophic."

"The Israeli PM?"

"In the dark. Real local cowboy that Intelligence Minister. He said that if the PM is made aware he will find it difficult to steer things in our direction with the US President."

"Reliable?"

"Who knows with these—" he was about to say something he would regret and stopped himself.

"Okay I will liaise with this… this Sammy character."

"Good," he said as Stamper stood up and grabbed his briefcase. "Oh and Stamper?"

"Yeah?"

"Shut the door after you please. Cheers, old boy."

It was a very loud bang indeed.

Chapter 11
Grosvenor Square, Mayfair

Sammy Zcharya sat on a bench in the heart of Grosvenor Square. The sky was painted white, and the air was chilling. He thought it was funny that Paris had essentially the same weather, yet somehow London was always considered bleaker and colder.

He reached down to his pocket and took out a packet of extra strength paracetamol tablets. He popped out two and put them in his mouth, swallowing hard with no water. This entire ordeal was giving him a headache which had started aboard the Eurostar.

He had tried to arrange a meeting with Langley's station in London, but was denied. He stared at the huge golden eagle, perched on the roof of the iconic American embassy building. He felt nothing but bitterness towards the ungrateful Americans. Aren't there when you need them, but sure to pass judgement when you don't.

His phone buzzed somewhere; he could feel the entire bench vibrating. He was annoyed at the fact that he had left it parked on his folded trench coat in such a distance that it could have easily been swiped. You are getting careless, Sammy dear, he thought to himself as he reached out and picked it up.

"Go ahead."

"I just had a call back from Langley." It was Edo Yichie, a low grade analyst from his Tel Aviv office, assigned to be his base support man for this mission. The guy was young, in his late twenties, too young for Sammy's liking. Although, admittedly, Sammy had left Paris in such a rush, that he could use both Edo's secretarial services as well as his technical abilities. The days of being alone in the field, even in a friendly environment, were over.

"Well go on!" he snapped.

"They don't acknowledge your authority to act on the matter; they think the Brits need to clean up their own backyard themselves – those were the analyst's exact words."

"So they sent a low grade guy to give you a cold shoulder…" he muttered.

"With all due respect, sir, it's not like a director is going to pick up when I ring. I'm surprised they even returned my call."

"Of course they did, because if this plays out like we originally planned with the Brits, be sure they will want to be in on the goods. They wouldn't distance themselves completely."

"I see."

"We learned one more thing though."

"Oh?"

"Whoever had given the go ahead for this thing from the start, at their end, was doing so on their own accord. We would not get them to admit they were in, which means that if push comes to shove, we'd better disappear quietly and let the Brits take the fallout."

"Okay, is there something else you need me to do?"

"I'll need a quick getaway route from this country, preferably one that can accommodate two people."

"Two?" Edo was perplexed.

"We don't know what the kid knows, and if I can't get him to cooperate... Well... let's just say I may need to carry my sick relative with me back to Israel."

"Understood, sir. I'm on it."

Sammy ended the call without even a word of thanks. The ultimate message from the Americans was 'play your cards right' and we shall meet afterwards. So there it was, as always he was expected to clean up the mess. He would have to meet with the Brits, just to see that they were on the same page. He had given the Minister for Intelligence Matters his personal assurance that the situation could be salvaged. Then the Minister would update the Israeli PM who would only be made aware once they were on top of things. It was meant to be a perfect plan. Now, he needed to speak to this boy Yochanan and knock some sense into him, or handle him differently, should this be required. He hoped it wasn't – he was getting too old for the physical side of this job. If only they had called him sooner; this would have already been under wraps.

He looked at the embassy's rectangular building again, such a shame that the Americans are moving to Battersea Park... Oh well, I guess it would mark an end of an era. Another era. He had seen so many now, he'd lost count. He lifted his head, this time the golden eagle was looking at him; his gaze judgmental and sinister.

Chapter 12
The Monument

Grey left John by the Monument. It was a peculiar landmark, he thought, as he was contemplating the golden sphere shaped like a burning urn at the top of two hundred foot stone obelisk. He was standing right by the entrance to the Underground, his gaze was occasionally disturbed by the passing pedestrians on the street. It was a small paved cul-de-sac with a concrete blockade placed at its edge. He could spot Grey making his way back. He had a duffle bag and was wearing a rather grim looking face. "The place has been ransacked. I don't think they took anything except for your laptop, which I couldn't find."

"Damn! They must have taken it! It was right on the dining table. Shit! There's nothing on it that can help them!"

"Finch just texted my burner." He was referring to a mobile phone that one would throw away after it was used for operational purposes. "It seems that they called off the chase for now. I wouldn't count on it though and I wouldn't want you to spend the night in your flat."

"But the fact that they aren't looking for us any more… it's a good sign, no?" His expression was hopeful.

"Until we get to the bottom of this I wouldn't crack open the champagne quite yet."

John nodded.

"We have two adjacent rooms booked in the Millennium Mayfair under Mr Ray Suarez, but don't attempt to check in on your own, they may require some sort of identification. Let's meet at the hotel bar around nine, I ought to have sorted it by then."

He nodded again, his eyes still focusing above Grey's head on the top of the monument. Grey handed him the bag and in a swift stride vanished into the station.

Not knowing what to do with himself he started heading west on Cannon Street, duffle bag in hand. Splashes of raindrops started prickling his face. It wasn't pouring hard enough for him to need a shelter, but the sensation of walking inside a field of small sprinklers was irritating. The streets were almost empty, and a red double-decker splashed his trousers with grey filthy puddle water.

He walked along King William Street and passed the Royal Exchange and the Bank of England. As he reached Moorgate, he lowered his eyes to the pavement, spotting perfect black imprints of the last of the autumn leaves, engraved by the combination of wetness and cold temperatures. Slowly but surely the city was drenched, but he paid no attention. He thought the shimmering waters on the ancient cobblestones were beautiful and his gaze was transfixed on the small speckles of light that they reflected. He took a hard left into Colman Street Buildings passage, where he halted under the multiple arched corridor, taking shelter from the now heavy rain. He couldn't help the notion that someone was hawking him, their gaze tearing a hole in his back. That disturbing premonition made him start walking again.

Admittedly, he was lost. The City of London could be a labyrinth of streets entwined among themselves in a web that had been woven for over half a millennium. Mason Avenue was one of these veins, the Old Doctor Butler's Head pub was very much inviting behind the screen of raindrops but he kept walking straight past, gliding on the crooked cobblestone pavements.

He strayed in the City's alleys until he reached Guildhall. The medieval-designed building seemed to him like a huge brick-made crown. The drops were falling on Guildhall's heavy wooden arched doors, making intense banging sounds, yet the doors seemed dry and unaffected. He wiped his face for no particular reason, it remained wet all the same. He stood alone in the centre of the square, trying to get the rain to wash some sense into current events. Had he been dreaming? Would he wake up tomorrow in his comfortable flat to another day of dreary IT work? The sensation that there were numerous eyes on him wouldn't let go, even in this exposed and deserted square. He briskly turned, spinning waves of water all around, expecting to find someone or something scrutinizing him. There was no one there.

Chapter 13
Mayfair

He emerged out of the Bond Street station, wet to the bone. It was hot and clammy underground, and the hike in the brick maze which is Bond Street station had left him short of breath. The events of the day were starting to take their toll, and he wore a mixture of rainwater and sweat odours. He punched in the Millennium Mayfair's address on the Google Maps App on his phone and headed left according to the painted instructions.

He kept walking along Gilbert Street. It was a narrow street with old style scarlet coloured brick mansion houses on both sides of it. Some of their ground floors were painted white. The small lattices were also painted white.

In the meanwhile, Liz's instructions were pretty straight forward: keep John Daniel in sight until further notice. It was quite difficult tracking him down again, but once Grey's visage was matched by the CCTV facial recognition software, it was only a matter of time before she was back on the trail.

It was silly of the old spymaster to go back to a place so obvious as the guy's apartement. Albeit she was not a part of the team that stormed his flat practising zero subtlety, she was kept in the loop and managed to hack into the live CCTV feed of the complex. After she located the duo in the city, she was compelled to follow him in the bloody rain and through the Tube ride all the way to Mayfair. She managed to stay unspotted and found a hidden corner in Grosvenor Square, from which she had a perfect 360-degree vantage point of the area. Her newly devised plan seemed bulletproof: since Grey foolishly disappeared, she would engage the guy and sit with him for a drink. She would try to learn about their next move, and plant a homing device on him. She was about to leave the safety of her corner when she noticed an old white-haired man with a grey trench coat initiating contact with her subject.

Sammy intercepted him in the middle of Grosvenor Square's green, as John was walking and looking at his phone at the same time. The green was pitch black, save a small area around the lamp posts, which produced a non illuminating white aura. John realized that the Millennium Mayfair was dead ahead, as he was walking south on the green's mid footpath. He then lifted his gaze and nearly bashed into the white-haired man.

"I'm sorry, mate," he managed to say while trying to balance himself in order to avoid the collision, losing his grip of the path in the process and nearly falling over. The man was substantially older than him but 'mate' was a safe choice in England.

The man responded with familiarity as if John was supposed to know him from somewhere. "Don't be," he said, then he switched to Hebrew and continued, *"You shouldn't be sorry, I'm here to help."*

"Who are you?" John's tone was suspicious and he seemed annoyed.

"The embassy sent me, just call me Sammy."

"Are you stalking me?"

"No, no, not at all," the man chuckled. *"I'm here to get you out of the predicament you're in."*

"And what predicament is that exactly?"

"We are both well aware of what you are involved with, Mr Daniel." He paused and scrutinized John from head to toe, then nodded with his eyes closed trying to show empathy to his shabby appearance. He then continued, *"Let's drop the charades, I work for the consul general, I can help."*

"What do you suggest?"

"Come back with me to the embassy, we'll fix you a bed for the night, we'll make some calls tomorrow and sort this with the SIS."

Sammy grinned. He looked sincere enough, but it was either that or he was the world's greatest liar, John thought. It would be nice to have this thing behind him. He reflected for a moment when a sudden warning bell started chiming in his head. The SIS… the SIS?! How could the guy possibly know that the SIS were involved?

"I think you are confusing me with someone else." He wore a straight face as he switched to English.

Sammy had imagined this would be difficult, but he hoped the soft persuasion would be enough. He guessed somewhere along his pitch he managed to mess it up and make the kid over-suspicious. It had started to seem to him that the kid was far more involved than what the English had realized. At the moment though he was compelled to let it go if he wanted the young man to ever regain a shred of trust in him. He cursed himself for not having the proper time to better prepare but knew that he must bite the bullet so to speak, at least for the time being.

He reached deep into his pocket and produced a business card. He handed it over to John.

"Suit yourself, Yochanan," he switched to English as well but referred to John by his proper Hebrew name. "Give me a call if you decide you need our help nonetheless."

John did not have the time to acknowledge the offer and Sammy was already brushing past him on his way to the green's north-east exit.

Could he have been wrong? Was the guy truly sincere? He was starting to have doubts as he lifted his hand that was tightly holding the business card. It read *'Samuel Z, Consular Assistance'*. There was no symbol or country flag, and the number was definitely not local.

Sammy Zcharya was quick to disappear to the safety of Davies Street shadows. He eyed a black-haired woman that was watching them from the corner of the green, hidden behind the benches. Yes, little if anything at all escaped Sammy's attentive eyes. In all of his years as an operative, he learned to notice each and every detail, as negligible as it may seem to anyone else.

He caught the Jubilee Line to Westminster station, and ascended in the escalator to change lines towards High Street Kensington. As he waited out the escalator ride, he reflected on what needed to be done in order to get on Yochanan Daniel's good side. He would learn from his improvisation fiasco, and prepare a small team from the local embassy employees. Edo would handle the details from Tel Aviv: nothing fancy, just a group of people that can provide logistic and administrative support for extraction. Second, he would update the head of the local Mossad station. He loved the respect he was getting from regional Mossad heads of stations, he was thriving on it. He was used to having them attend to his every need, and expected nothing less than a hundred per cent of the resources they had at their disposal. In all his years as an operative in Europe, Sammy had made a name for himself as being Mossad's 'cleaner' – its on-call problem solver. He was based in Paris since the late eighties, running his autonomous espionage kingdom from there. He was notorious in most of Europe's intelligence services, and during the late nineties became a *persona non grata* in England.

As he was just making it to the District Line, he reflected on the events that kept him from returning to London in the past two decades. In 1998 an extreme Imam called Abdulla Rahim had been assassinated in his house in Luton. It was the last two years of the worst Labour government in terms of attitude towards Israel. In fact, Rahim was engaged not only in massive Muslim propaganda, but also Mossad had tangible evidence that he was using his rights as a religious community pillar in Britain to actively fund terror acts in Europe. They could specifically connect him to an armed assault on a synagogue in Marseille that saw three fatalities, and a few anti-Semitic crimes in London as well. With the British government refusing to put an end to Rahim's activities, Mossad stepped in. The problem was that the three agents that had been involved were caught by the British police forces as they were trying to flee the country. They were put on a mock trial that lasted nearly two years, with the charges finally dropped only when the Conservatives took power, and after intense pressure from the United States. The three, even though not officially found guilty in a British court of law, were then deported, and Sammy who had been accused of perverting the course of justice during their trial, shared the same retribution. He had not been seen in the UK since.

There was one consensus within the global intelligence community: if old Sammy was involved, there would not be any evidence linking the Israelis to the given event. He would shamelessly use fake passports, whether they were Australian or Canadian, or any other Israeli ally – he had the whole repertoire in store. He made witnesses disappear or retract their testimony, and he would not stop at anything trying to keep his agents safe.

In recent years, partly thanks to the American-Iranian nuclear détente, the relationship between Mossad and MI6 warmed up. It was an open secret that MI6 and the Conservative government would do anything to stop these talks and will push to restore the sanctions on Iran. Strangely enough the majority in the CIA shared their views. Rumours said that Langley, or at least a prominent faction of it, went rogue against their own Commander-In-Chief, and were covertly supporting the British. When Mossad was asked in on the ploy, and agreed to play along despite the Israeli PM's refusal, Sammy was immediately briefed. He strongly agreed that the talks must end and enthusiastically committed himself to this cause. Now it seemed that the Americans were getting cold feet. Never mind. He would not let something as puny as a clueless boy ruin the relationship renaissance he was enjoying with the British SIS. Not this time round.

Chapter 14
Whitehall

The little library in the MoD's main building that served as the Secretary's cigar room never looked gloomier. The overhead lights had stopped working due to some electrical fault, which occurred every once in a while due to the building's advanced age. Despite the Secretary's explicit orders, the electricians could not get the lights back on.

The massive building had been built over two decades, between the thirties and the late fifties, and all the handymen agreed between themselves that only a monumental refurbishment would manage to re-illuminate the ancient library. Meanwhile, three impressively colourful Tiffany lamps were brought in from the basement in order to shed some light for the three o'clock brandy and cigars. Little did the maintenance guys know that these lamps were worth tens of thousands of pounds, and one got negligibly scratched in the moving process.

"Barbaric," said Sir Willow, as he was sipping an XO Courvoisier cognac from a crystal chalice. He was slouched in a heavy leather green sofa-chair that matched the room's darkness as well as the heavy-set dark wooden bookcase. He was pointing at the deep scratch that was apparent on the standing Tiffany lamp. Its shade was a mosaic of grey, green and red butterfly-shaped crystals. It was extraordinary.

Old Sir Willow was seventy-three, bulky, with a big paunch sticking out of his bespoke Henry Poole Prince of Wales style suit. He was very much accustomed to luxury and his drooping bulldog cheeks were solid proof of that.

"Yes, yes, truly savages," mocked Ian Collinson, the PM's chief of staff, who was holding a glass of cognac of his own.

Collinson was forty-four years old, had dark grey hair and was balding at the top. He was of average height and sturdy-built, but with a small paunch. He was serving as the PM's chief of staff since his re-election. Prior to that he was the Tories' chief strategist and campaign manager. He took the helm of what seemed to be a lost campaign, half-way through. He was nicknamed 'Mister Fix-it' after he managed to shift public opinion and erase a twelve points trail to the Labour party. The campaign he'd led was ruthless and full of smearing that peaked with the release of tapes proving the Labour candidate's sordid rapports with the heads of the country's most prominent union representatives. The election ended with a needle-thread win by the Conservatives, which called for a coalition government with the Lib Dems. But this of course was the lesser of two evils, since the Tories were left the ruling party for the next five years. Collinson was also the head of the coalition negotiations. He was a shrewd negotiator, and managed to retain the Foreign and Defence ministries in the hands of the Conservatives, as well as the Exchequer. The position of the PM's Chief of Staff was his reward for a job well done.

The door to the library opened slowly and Olly Jones was quick to pass through it, closing it swiftly behind him to leave the room in its darkness.

"Why is it so dark in here?" he asked.

"Ah young, Olly!" Sir Willow cried. "Nice of you to join us, fix you a drink, old boy?"

"Thanks but I'll pass, I still have a long day ahead."

"Of course, of course." Sir Willow nodded. The old Secretary always seemed like his mind was otherwise occupied with different matters.

"What did the PM say?" Olly turned to Collinson. There was always tension between the two, although it was mellowed down by a feeling of mutual respect. Collinson knew that Olly Jones' head spun around intelligence and foreign affairs and that he was not very politics-savvy. He appreciated it, and decided it would better serve to keep him close, perhaps nurture him to a future political candidacy.

"He said you should come in and see him first thing tomorrow morning at Number Ten. He is not impressed."

"Yes but what does he—"

"I'm just the messenger, Olly. I have no take on the matter."

"Of course… of course…" Willow mumbled.

"Nonetheless, surely he told you what he thinks." Olly hated the fact that Collinson was already preparing for some future investigation committee. If nothing else, Collinson would be remembered as the one with no take on this matter, he was simply delivering the message. Great help. Gee, thanks, mate, he thought to himself.

"He only said that if they – I mean the White House – found out that we are in bed with the Israelis, the shit'll hit the fan."

"Well, that's alread—" he was interrupted.

"He thinks that both the White House and the Israeli PM would leak it, as the best possible means to distance themselves from it."

"And Langley's involvement? He is aware that this was coordinated initially with the boys at Grosvenor Square, right?"

"He fears that this would never come out, that they'll deny unambiguously."

"This can bring the coalition down…" muttered Willow.

"Not anything we didn't know beforehand," Olly responded to both.

"But maybe something we should have gravely considered before stepping into such an ordeal," Collinson shot back.

"Policy isn't set according to polls and public opinion!"

"On the contrary!" Collinson raised his voice.

"Gents!" Sir Willow interrupted the verbal duel. "How we reached this situation is water under the bridge."

Both of them remained silent, they were well aware that there would be plenty of time to assign guilt later on and that Willow was correct in stating the need to try and find a pre-emptive solution.

"I want you to put your heads together and find the best way of dealing with the current situation, presuming it will come out some way or another. We also have to consider the Israeli PM, if he finds out sooner than we realize he may blow this up just to draw the fire away from him – in which case we will be in a pickle. A rather big one if I may add."

Collinson chugged down the rest of his cognac with a big slurp. "Surely he doesn't want to see the only supporting European government he has fall, now does he?" Collinson asked the centre of the room, his face already red from the alcohol.

"I am not entirely sure he would assess our predicament so accurately," Olly volunteered an answer as Willow was busy refreshing his drink.

"Of course…" Willow mumbled.

"The Israelis aren't big on British politics," Olly continued. "In the US they have AIPAC to protect their interests. In England public opinion is much more ambiguous. They will make do with another Labour government if they have to."

"Erm…" Willow half coughed.

"I see," Collinson said.

"Are there any incriminating documents bearing our signatures?" Willow asked the two, sounding sharper than ever.

"Nothing from the PM's office," Collinson was quick to answer.

"But there could be from the ministry or SIS." Olly looked away.

"Nasty business," whispered Sir Willow.

"Can we get on top of this thing?" asked Collinson.

"I'll work my press connections, see if anyone leaks something, it better not be linked straight to Downing Street in any event. I'll handle it," Olly volunteered.

"Are you still in that journalist's good books? What's her name…?" Collinson was well aware of the rumours involving their relationship.

"Katie Jones. And yes I am. I try and throw an exclusive her way every now and then, helps me when I need us to look good in the press."

"Call her up, open a good Châteauneuf-du-Pape."

"To what end?"

"Have her check their sources, if anyone implied—"

"Wouldn't we be rattling the cages unnecessarily? Someone may start digging because we started to ask questions."

"If she finds something I'd rather it be her, we'll get her to drop it, no?" Collinson motioned his glass towards Willow, who was more than ready to pour the younger man a new drink.

"She's like a dog with a bone, if she finds something she'll never drop it."

"Even at the cost of an exclusive with the PM?"

"Depends."

"Depends on what?" Willow raised his eyebrows.

"If she smells blood or not…"

"Well, it's up to you to confuse her sense of smell." Collinson winked and pulled half a smile.

Olly hated his style, but had to admit the man had a point. The only way of finding out if they were out of the woods was by doing some digging themselves and not leaving it all to Stamper and his men, who would do everything possible to cover up their own mistakes.

"Did you talk to Stamper?" Willow asked.

"Yeah, I made sure that he understands he has one chance of making this right."

"How did he take it? I reckon not too well," Collinson asked, taking another big swig from the glass.

"He tried to threaten us back. I set him straight."

"The nerve…" Willow shook his head.

"I have such a big dossier on him, if he even tries pointing fingers we'll finish him off. His picture will be in every tabloid," Collinson said with resolution. He got up and left the empty cognac glass on a small wooden table. "Gentlemen, if you'll excuse me." He started making his way towards the door, lingering just enough to allow one of the two to ask him the eminent question.

"Ian." It was Willow who stepped up.

"Yes, sir?"

"Do you think we can get away with it?"

"I am certain we won't…" and he had left the room.

Chapter 15
Moscow 1991

Yeltsin's tanks were still parked up around the Red Square. It had been two days of quiet in Moscow, during which people refrained from leaving their homes. Two days that made the Russian capital seem like a ghost city. The sun washed over the Kremlin buildings and the White House, the Russian parliament building. Her rays jumped off the armoured vehicles, emphasizing the spectrum festival that was St Basil's Cathedral and its proximate buildings. It was placid and hard to imagine that only two days before, an epic standoff had taken place in that exact spot.

The masses that had been occupying the Red Square for the past days were gone, and even though the country was in chaos, the queues to the grocery stores and bread shops were relatively light. Everybody was well aware that Gorbachev's resignation would bring the country to a standstill, but the Russian sense of patience and calmness prevailed. It was earlier that day that Gorbachev announced the formation of the 'Committee for the Operational Management of the

Soviet Economy', the first sign of life from the crippled Russian government.

Nikolayev was among the few that remained bunched outside the Kremlin building. Like many of the top ranking KGB officers, he chose to leave his uniform at home and was wearing a set of raggedy-looking civilian clothes. As the future was uncertain, like many of his peers, he made sure not to go back to his office at the Lubyanka building, fearful that high ranking military officials would get arrested. It was apparent to everyone that the military would keep its grip on the matters of state for the meanwhile, but there was no telling to what extent the executive officials would try to appease the West. Going about with prudence was wise. Shady characters, that were associated with the darker side of the party, may be paraded as scapegoats, and Nikolayev wasn't going to make it easier on them to include him on those lists. He waited. He was looking for news, trying to read between the lines. He kept trying to gain access to his small secondary office in the Kremlin, desperate to catch a glimpse of a telegram or a fax that would scatter the mist of the future of Mother Russia.

He thought about simply running away when it was reported that the attempted coup by 'the Gang of Eight' had failed. He couldn't stop wondering what could have happened had they had the sense to detain that degenerate Yeltsin when he was out of the country. How underestimating your adversary could bring down plans that held the fate of millions. He was quite certain that the incumbent Prime Minister Silayev wouldn't have had the guts to oppose them on his own. "Bunch of morons," he cursed to himself reflecting on the events that got him to be standing like a beggar in the Moscow cold.

Bigger crowds of people were gathering by the fences to watch a news van's small TV screen that was broadcasting the funeral of the three soldiers who had died trying to hold back the revolutionary forces. Yeltsin was giving an enrapturing speech in which he declared that Gorbachev would be awarded the Hero of the State medal. Welcome the age of Russian free politics, he thought to himself.

Colonel Professor Vasiliy Nikolayev walked away from the crowd with his back turned away from the Kremlin building. As he went past a news van someone grabbed him from behind and poked his back with a hard metal object. "*Keep walking, Colonel,*" the guy whispered in foreign-accented Russian. He swallowed hard. The moment he feared most had arrived. If he was exposed right here and now as a KGB officer, there was no telling what the enchanted mob would do to him. They would rip him apart. He could not turn his head to see his tormentor, yet something in his voice seemed familiar. He kept the same pace as before and walked towards the centre of Red Square, where only a few people were passing by. It was then when he managed to pivot himself and face his abductor face to face. He was familiar alright: with his high forehead, dark hair and apathetic gaze Jamie Jensen was certainly someone Nikolayev didn't expect to find in this place at this combustible time.

"What takes you out of the warmth of the corner office, Agent Jensen? MI6 are missing some field operatives perhaps?" Nikolayev tried to mask the tension.

Jensen slid his Walther back inside his coat and lit a Woodbine cigarette, English made, Nikolayev noticed, impossible to come across in the crumbling USSR. "Desperate times require desperate means, old boy." He motioned the pack towards Nikolayev, who at his turn pulled out a cigarette and accepted a light from Jensen's silver Ronson.

"So what does Her Majesty wants from me?" Nikolayev asked as he inhaled the sweet smoke of the English cigarette, this was heaven compared to the Soviet junk he was given from the party. Ex party.

"Not us, the Americans."

"You working for the Yanks now?"

"Not quite."

"Then what is it?"

"I was asked to arbitrate a deal with you on their behalf; it's an offer you couldn't possibly refuse."

"As you see my stack is not very big at the moment, go on…" Nikolayev could not hide the excitement in his eyes, there wouldn't be a single man that would dare call him a traitor if he accepted a deal from Langley nowadays!

"Easy now…" Jensen stubbed the cigarette and lit up a second. A bystander was waiting for the two to move on, and when they didn't, he un-hesitantly shot in and lifted the used stub from the floor only to clear the area straight away.

"I am here to tell you that you need to decline," Jensen continued.

"Oh?"

"Is there a café or a Russian tea house around here? I am dying for a cuppa."

"Where do you think you are, Agent Jensen? Can't you smell the blood around you? There isn't a coffee shop open in the entire land. For twenty years now you couldn't get real coffee in Moscow if your life depended on it. Now focus, I gather you didn't fly all the way here to discuss the failure of Bolshevism; what do the Americans offer? Why would I possibly decline it?"

They started pacing side by side like old schoolmates.

"The future, Colonel." He deliberately used his rank. "There's a lot of pressure from everyone to take the KGB apart. Yeltsin, Gorbachev or whoever is going to try and salvage what's left of this bullshit you guys call an economy will have to resort to drastic measures… Reforms. That's if they would want the West to help. Intelligence, KGB, it's all gone bye-bye, comrade."

Jensen's little teasing irritated him. But then again, he knew that he had a point. Soon enough the high ranking intelligence officers would have to pay their pound of flesh. He was in no position to refuse anything that Jensen was offering. Maybe he could sweeten the deal though.

"The Americans want all the high ranking First Chief Directorate officers sent to Langley. They want to know exactly in what stage your nuclear program is, and who is going to sell secrets to new enemy states. I was supposed to deliver you."

"Why can't they do it themselves?"

"Joint venture I suppose. Or so they sold to my superiors. In any event, that's immaterial."

"Oh?"

"Yeah, since you are going to refuse and I will deliver them your lieutenant instead."

"Ivanovic is useless! He will get you nowhere." His blood was starting to boil.

"I know, old sport – you are the real deal." Jensen's tone was appeasing but he was as mocking as ever. "Don't worry, we'll give them Ivanovic as the little fish while I tell them that you refused to play ball."

"And why would I refuse? I don't follow…"

"Because of our new joint venture."

"KGB and MI6?"

Jensen laughed. "Jensen et Nikolayev Ltd."

"Oh?"

"I'll get you out of here, old boy, the highest bidder is currently the Pakistanis but the North Koreans are in a strong second."

"You made contact with them?" Nikolayev was perplexed at Jensen's insinuations; he would never have guessed him to be a traitor.

"Through mediators."

"And if it's an entrapment?"

"Then we have a lot to lose," he managed a fake laugh.

"How are you planning on pulling this off?"

"Simple enough, you're going to run and I will be forced to kill you."

Nikolayev opened his eyes in astonishment.

"You'll lay low, and I'll keep monitoring the grapevine. If someone's on to us, I'll find out soon enough."

"You have a destination in mind?"

"I have a good contact in the Syrian Military Intelligence, a chap we tried turning a few years back. He'll keep you safe for a year, for the right fee."

"Let me think about it?"

"I'm off this cuckoo nest on the 8 pm flight to London. Your call whether you'll be riding in the trunk or alongside me."

"Jensen?"

"Yes, old boy."

"Not many people have threatened me and lived to tell. If I choose to go along, it's only because at the moment it seems that it's my best option to get out of here in one piece."

"Yes of course, old boy. But I have a feeling that once the money'll start flowing you're gonna thank me."

As soon as he had arrived home, Nikolayev hastily packed a suitcase. Save a few diagrams and some discs he had managed to salvage from his office, it was all inconsequential. The little items that he packed were not of great significance as long as he had his best weapon at hand – his brains. Everything else would save a few weeks of work – but nothing too crucial. As he was packing he couldn't help but reflect about the life of the little boy Vasiliy, who dreamt about becoming a cosmonaut, fuelled by stories of the space heroes of the Soviet Union. That little boy was physically too weak to be considered as a candidate for the Red Star space camp, but would otherwise prove his worth with his mind, by constantly being the top of his class and by excelling in his academic studies.

These years of endearing support from the party had helped shape the man Vasiliy had become and brought him to where he was today: the youngest man to ever have spearheaded the Soviet nuclear program. However, with everything he had ever known crumbling down, it was time for Nikolayev to take action. Jensen was a product of the capitalistic system, he was not to be blamed. If anything, his sense of greed, rather than duty, had arrived in Moscow just in time. It was a fair assumption that anyone else would have just thrown him to the hands of the Americans, then he would have been compelled to work for the capitalists. Jensen, who he had met in the past, was a godsend! In his heart he knew that he would return to Moscow in the future.

He would bide his time and come back at the right time, for the right reasons. And when he did, he would get a welcome saved for heroes of the revolution, after he had made the world pay dearly for what was done to the Russian people.

Chapter 16
Katie

Katie woke up and slowly opened her eyes. Through the open blinds of her bedroom she could see that the London sky was already painted in dark blue, a typical colour for the English morning skyline in the cold months. She squinted through her wavy brown hair that was unkempt from the night's tossing and turning, and switched her gaze towards the man that was dressing next to her.

"What time is it? Leaving already?"

"Quarter to six. Yes, the office called, the PM is up and wants me in a meeting scheduled for 7 am."

"Impressive for a civil servant," she giggled and sat up.

"No rest for the wicked, Katie, who knows it better than you?" he smirked and went into the bathroom.

The two bedroom flat, in a divided old Victorian semidetached house in Holland Park, was Katie Jones' crown jewel. At thirty-five years of age, the ambitious young reporter was unattached, and constantly chasing the next political scoop, and could not be bothered with an ongoing relationship or men in general.

Olly Jones was her soft belly, her kryptonite. Since the two had met at a reception held in Downing Street four years ago – she could not resist him. It all started as a casual fling that emerged from a flirtatious conversation about their shared last name, despite their two dichotomist backgrounds. Him – the poster boy of the English private education, with an ultra-wealthy family, royally titled and properties in northern England; Her – a daughter to a Jewish single mother from north London and a black-English father, who took off when she was only a toddler. She was a product of a hard childhood with a mother who was always juggling two jobs. Her parents' divorce became final when she was three, and she never kept in touch with her dad, blaming him for caving in to the pressure made by his family, which eventually drove him to give up on her and her mum. She heard that he was remarried with children, but she had no interest to make contact.

She had made a name for herself as a reporter when she exposed a corruption scandal that involved a few senior parliamentarians. In the following year, she had received the Orwell prize for excellence in journalism and the British press award. Since then she had become the most sought after journalist in the land. She became the *Telegraph*'s senior political correspondent, a change that had improved her work conditions immensely. She had managed to afford a down payment on the expensive Holland Park flat, and in general started compensating for the small things she had missed growing up: designer clothes and expensive shoes among others.

During the years that followed the scoop that had made her, she built a reputation as someone who didn't run from any story, no matter how dark and twisted it may be. She had already received many threatening letters during the years, but these seemed only to encourage her.

The fact that Olly was married with two small children didn't make her walk away. Whenever he called she was ready, no emotional drama to follow and no commitment requirements. At first she made the excuse that he was a good leaping board to advance her career. But as time went by, even the excuses seemed redundant. He had such a hold on her that she simply wouldn't resist him. Couldn't. Didn't want to.

Olly came out of the bathroom, sat on the end of the bed and put on his black Grenson shoes. When he had called last night, she was already half dressed for bed, after having two glasses of red wine with her takeaway curry dinner. As always, he was waiting on the front lawn when he rang her… 'I could have been with someone' she had told him, as she unlocked the front door.

He stepped into the other room and she could soon hear her Nespresso coffee machine at work.

"You'd better be making me a cup as well!" she hollered above the machine's intolerable noise.

He came into the room with two steaming espresso cups. As she took the cup from his hand she gave him a harsh look.

"Half a spoon of sugar?" using her most inquisitive voice. He just smiled and leaned to kiss her on the forehead.

"I'll be in touch soon," he said, downed the rest of his coffee and rushed to the living room. She was putting in her contact lenses as she heard the front door closing behind him.

She reflected on last night as she was sipping her strong espresso. After they'd had sex, he wanted to come clean and started explaining that his visit was not all pleasure. He told her what he needed her to do for him.

"I wasn't aware that I am now working as a researcher for the PM's office," she had told him.

He had frowned. "You will benefit from this."

"You are asking me to work against my journalistic integrity. What is it that I'm meant to be looking for anyway?"

"Dear, if I'd tell you, I might as well read it on the front cover of the *Sunday Times*." He deliberately used the name of her number one rival.

"So what's the deal?" she had asked, she could hardly refuse him.

"When you tell me what you have managed to find out you buy yourself the scoop and the exclusive with the PM to follow. If you tell me that *The Times* or anyone else has it I'll make sure you get it before them."

They needed the ability to contain the story, not looking to censor it he had explained, but she couldn't remember his exact words now.

She pulled her iPad from below the bed and started searching the news feeds. Something to do with MoD, he wouldn't tell her what. She suddenly felt cheap. She composed herself and threw the duvet off. "Olly Jones, you're in for a big surprise."

***

As he was driving his small Golf, Olly Jones felt a sense of accomplishment. He smiled to himself when thinking back on how he managed to spin things over. Still something felt amiss. He was not a hundred per cent sure that Katie had bought it, at the smell of a scoop she would probably say just about anything. He punched in Collinson's number on the mobile phone, then changed his mind and tossed the device to the passenger's seat. As he took a hard right on to Park Lane he noticed that the road was nearly empty and then laid his foot heavily on the accelerator pedal.

Chapter 17
Belsize Park

Saturday morning was quite placid. Jamie Jensen, having arrived home at 2 am, allowed himself a lay in. His wife tried to wake him up to go out with his twin girls, as they were home from uni for the weekend, but he waved her off and just kept on sleeping. As soon as he heard the front door closing, he allowed himself to wake up. Undisturbed he tried to make coffee in his expensive Elektra machine, only to discover that it was still broken. He was in a foul mood. "Sodding coffee machine and sodding wife that does absolutely nothing in this house," he cursed to himself.

As the years went by Jensen started feeling like he was losing his grip. First his family life – with the girls out in Brighton doing God knows what, then his aging body that was betraying him bit by bit. Now it was the grip on his job, with C riding him hard yesterday night.

He dressed up in informal clothes – blue jeans and a grey dress shirt, and wore a light blue sweater on top. Later he would drop by the office and see what more Agent Shaw could find. He had to admit that she was good, far better than the apes from the Increment. He had no problem using either of the two departments for a UK based mission. Normally any mission that was to take place on British soil required special approvals from the Joint Intelligence Committee, JIC. There were however a handful of people that could sigh off such activities, provided they could justify it later. That was, if inquired, as C always added. Jensen was one of them. In retrospect, it was a silly decision to activate the Increment, they lacked the subtleness that agents who were long trained in Ops, like Liz Shaw, had. He cursed himself for making the wrong choice. While the Increment provided muscles over brains, Ops provided quality work. They were briefly nicknamed 'The Lamplighters' when the John le Carré books became popular. It was he that put an end to that sad joke. His wife often accused him of lacking a sense of humour.

Back in the day, Jensen had grand plans for the service. After the disastrous eighties and the stagnated nineties, he truly thought that he could get the service back on its feet. The brass had different ideas. Stamper was the ultimate 'yes man' of the institution at the time. Having come from a family with royal connections gave him the final push. Jensen was left with the daydreams, and his current position, a pay grade good enough to prevent him from quitting. But the realization that he's on a slow train towards retirement and the ultimate decay that comes with it, helped shape the James Jensen he is today.

The north London neighbourhood of Belsize Park was very calm, as it would be on a Saturday morning. As he closed the front door to his semidetached house, he took in a breath full of cold crisp air. He was fastening his black Burberry coat as he took a right turn to England's Lane. It was a mixed street: on one end was a wild and ancient looking green, while on the other a row of classic white Victorian houses whose ground floors had been converted into very untidy shops, cafés and a Tesco. The street had only a handful of pedestrians walking about: a few mothers with prams and two guys tinkering underneath the hood of a parked Range Rover. As he walked towards the little café Ginger & White, he caught a glimpse of two men having a go at a waitress for not serving any morning liquors. "Idiots," he looked their way and muttered to himself. Wasting the sense of security given to them by devoted civil servants such as himself. No wonder we aren't an empire any longer, he thought to himself. It was injustices such as the Stamper appointment that, in his mind, justified him succumbing to temptations he had come across doing this job. The first time he had strayed was with the same Nikolayev that was making life difficult for him in the present day. He ended up getting paid handsomely by the Pakistanis for that. Ever since, he had a few more clandestine affairs that meant to make sure he would get the pension he truly deserved. 'The first sin is always the hardest' a blood diamonds dealer told him in Swaziland. As he gave the guy a nine millimetre bullet hole in the head, he reflected on that statement and disagreed. He thought that the older he got the harder it felt, if not conscience-wise, then at least in the operational aspect. He felt old.

He walked into Ginger & White and ordered a double espresso to go. He wanted to give the gentlemen who tormented the waitress a go, but by the time it was ready, the rowdy duo were gone. He put down the paper cup and tried reaching into his jacket's pocket in order to retrieve his cigarettes. Instead he found an electronic pen-shaped cigarette with a note bearing his wife's handwriting *'try this instead'*. He cursed and tucked the plastic cylinder back into his pocket. He picked up the coffee and walked down the street.

In the corner of the street, past the Tesco, a man wearing a black down jacket and a grey old-styled hat was awaiting him. His visible hair was white, and he was holding a folded copy of the Saturday *Times*. Jensen took a large swig and tossed away the empty cup to a bin by the kerb.

"You'd better be more discrete; they stopped making hats like these somewhere in the middle of the last century." He scoffed at the man.

"I'll remember the advice, Jamie," the man dismissed his mockery.

Jensen didn't care for Sammy, his presence made him edgy. He still remembered the mess that this guy created in England back in the day. He was not a one to forgive and forget.

"Can you update me where things currently stand?" Sammy inquired impatiently.

"The only one that might presently tie us to Nikolayev is Adam Grey. Ever met him?"

"Yeah, smart guy. Our paths crossed in Berlin, before the wall fell. Not like the rest of the idiots you guys produce!"

Jensen let this one go. "Well, he only has the passports we tried arranging for the professor, but things escalated a bit; the brass are panicking."

"Can't you just pick him up?"

"C is afraid that it will expose us too much. Besides, I already tried and C nearly ordered my head put on a stick, some jackass started shooting around in Chelsea. Took a bit of persuasion to keep it off the news cycles."

"Yeah I was briefed." Sammy tried to convey the appearance like he wasn't paying too much attention, but

Jensen knew better. "I made contact with the lad yesterday, but I should've waited," he continued.

"Yes I was informed."

"The dark-haired girl. Yeah, she's cute."

"You made her?!" Jensen was perplexed. He knew that the old Mossad git was good, but Agent Shaw was one of the best they had.

Sammy smirked. "I doubt this kid has a clue what's at stake, and I trust your guys gave him a good fright, so he will probably stick to Grey now, I would have. On his own he wouldn't have posed a real threat. You guys got the British press covered?"

"The politicians are on top of this one. Won't be the first time they spin things their way with the press."

"What else?"

"If this gets out of hand, I have a proper distraction I can manifest. Everyone will be up to their necks with this mess, it will give us enough time to get Nikolayev where we need him."

"Make sure you do, I think we're already there. What is your impression regarding Langley?"

"They will only step in if they walk into the American embassy across from their hotel. Otherwise, they shan't get their handprint all over this. But I don't think we have to worry about that, it's not Grey's style to get help from the outside, he's a serviceman at heart."

"I had a chat with them myself." He lied.

"Oh?" Jensen tried to hide his irritation.

"Nothing concrete. But I think your small distraction is in order. I hope you understand the real cost of failure here, right?"

Jensen nodded. "We can contain it." Jensen hoped he sounded as sure as he tried to portray.

"Make the distraction, and go and visit your mate Nikolayev. We have a week and we need to signal the Americans to locate him in Teheran, it can't happen overnight or it will be too obvious."

"I'm aware of the timetable!" Jensen snapped, then shot Sammy a scrupulous look. It was bad enough that C made him work with a foreign service, he was not about to take orders from this man.

"I'll tie the loose ends here with the boy and fuck off; nobody could link it back to you that way."

They had been walking quite a while now on Primrose Hill Road, and Jensen stopped suddenly as he noticed the green lawns and the grassy hill of Primrose Hill.

Sammy was already leaning towards the road trying to hail a faraway cab. As the driver seemed like he had finally spotted him, he turned his head towards Jensen.

"Anything else?" Jensen coldly asked.

"Yes," Sammy said as the taxi pulled in front of them and he climbed to the back seat. "This time, don't fuck up!"

Screeching its wheels, the cab drove away.

Chapter 18
Olly

It was ten in the morning when Olly Jones slammed shut the door to their five bedroom flat in the Barbican Centre. He threw the keys on the coffee table and stared at the bourgeois Ikea furnished pale living room.

Buying this apartment was the long withheld fulfilment of a promise he gave his wife. It was only fair, as she had agreed to sacrifice her short term dreams when Olly first joined the ranks of the Tories. It was apparent then that the first years as a low ranking civil servant would not allow them the lavish life she had dreamt of, nor to own a property in central London like she desired. Political power and money may go together, but certainly not as a junior party member – not even a legislator yet. He had learned this first-hand when he filled positions such as a campaign surveyor, a parliamentary aide, an advisor to the Under-Secretary of Energy and even an aide to the Minister of State for Farming, Food and the Marine Environment, when times were especially rough. This impressive repertoire of roles, interesting as they may be, didn't exactly guarantee an affable relationship with one's banker, as he quickly discovered. His wife, having taken a timeout from her promising legal career in order to care for their children, never stopped showing her dissatisfaction from the two and then three bedroom flats they had rented on the fringes of the Tube map, during those years.

Six years ago, as the pressure took its toll, he decided to leave the idealism behind and take on a job as a PR officer in a media corporation. Only fate had its scheming way, and a chance meeting with the Secretary for Energy and Climate Change had shuffled the deck. Alongside today's PM, Olly went up in the ranks of the Conservatives. His appointment to the JISC, when the PM was still the Secretary of Defence, had made sure that his name would be commonly spoken among the party's elders. He had become a 'made man'.

Riding along with the PM, Jones had managed to play the homeland security maverick card ever since. He became the youngest man in the modern era to occupy the position of special advisor to the PM for State and Foreign Affairs, and one of the final rulers in matters of security and intelligence. The 'Position of Trust' came with many perks, one of which was a proper salary that helped him secure a mortgage for the luxurious apartment at the Barbican.

The bourgeois apartment, which was meticulously furbished, was now clad in an eye-soring mess generally produced by his two children, a girl aged eight and a boy aged six. Olly slid open the living room curtains, and stared out of the wall-size triple-glazed window. The Barbican complex that may have been glamorous at some point during the nineties, seemed to him like a big chunk of grey sooty cement. It was entwined with outdoors corridors and concrete staircases that made the design seem chaotic, and he couldn't master the passages even after three years of living there. He was scanning the Cromwell Tower that was to the right and his eyes kept gliding left where he could make out some of the City's protrusive buildings. He imagined the City rats pouring more oil to the axles of the financial juggernaut called the City of London. From his position, he knew that the UK's economy was ill. The latest governmental projections that were kept under wraps, pointed to a further decline in the GDP and a stagnating growth. He knew that if the coalition could survive the current crisis, by this time next year unemployment would soar and then the coalition would likely fail. For the first time in years, he was truly worried.

It was this exact economic nightmare that had him conceive the plan which was now set in motion. Drawing the attention back to Iran would resurface the homeland security card, in which the PM, thanks to him, was perceived by the public as quite strong. The consensus had been that Iran was indeed very near the point of no return in its nuclear program. The problem was that the American president was a big advocate of diplomacy, which in this case was a clear waste of time. The JIC had been shown reports indicating that in the very near future, the centrifuges in various locations in Iran would be operative. There was certainly no need for so many of these for peaceful nuclear purposes. The Ayatollahs were building the bomb.

There were even more reports that showed a full armed confrontation with ground troops dispatched to Iran would make the Afghanistan war seem like a neighbourhood knife fight. Even with the Americans leading a coalition force the casualties would be unbearable, in a way that would soon change public opinion.

The American State Department had read the same reports, and fearing an even greater decline in the president's popularity as a result from such a conflict, initiated the nuclear talks. Against all intelligence forecasts, the Iranians were keen to play ball or at least lead the Americans by the nose. Meanwhile a secret report issued by the MoD showed that with the Americans remaining neutral, a confrontation with Iran would be a regular Armageddon, whether it was led by Britain, the UN, Israel, the Saudis or any other coalition that would not involve the United States. There were further reports showing that such a conflict would raise the power of the quasi Islamic State.

The assessments had made this action clear: the nuclear talks must come to an end. The problem was that there was no intelligence backed proof to show the Americans that the Iranians were faking. And so a shady coalition was formed. The SIS agreed to carry out the plan, and after private talks that Stamper held with Langley it looked like the executive levels of both the CIA and Mossad would play ball despite it being against their governments' declared policies.

He sat down at his desk and switched on his PC. He started typing while reflecting on other intelligence reports he had seen as part of his JIC responsibilities. There were indications that Iran was funding Euro-based terrorist cells, aimed at raising havoc and chaos in the West should the nuclear talks end in an undesirable outcome. An insurance policy of some twisted sort. The problem was that it would be practically impossible to expose these cells without subjecting the citizens to the risk of an atrocious terrorist attack. Nobody was willing to go that far. Besides, these Iranian funded cells were monitored regularly, and unlikely to slip under the thumb on their own accord. As Collinson put it, public opinion is shaped by events and not by efficient grey work. While the intelligence branches' success in preventing hostile activities on British soil was superb, it would be the one event that had turned into a multiple casualty scene that had a remote chance to revise the American president's opinion.

As he finished typing the first letter, he saved it with the name 'press brief'. Then he made himself a cup of tea and started working on the second letter titled 'Dear Mr PM'. This would be his resignation letter, in which he took responsibility for the events that took place, though he didn't fully clear the PM. 'Good soldiers need to know how to fall on their swords' Sir Willow always said. However, Olly wasn't willing to give up his career so fast, and not this flat in the Barbican. He copied the two files to a disk-on-key, then deleted the original files from his hard drive. He hoped to God he would never have to use them.

Chapter 19
The Millennium Mayfair

John slept in late. At quarter past eleven Grey barged into his room with fresh coffee and croissants. He devoured them.

It was a slow Saturday. White clouds ruled the skyline, with spells of sun every now and then, which emphasized the bright green of Grosvenor Square. He turned away from the window and grabbed a bottle of sparkling water from the mini bar.

"We're on a budget you know," Grey protested. "I could have gotten you water from Tesco, I'm sure they would have tasted just the same for two quid less."

John gulped the bottle until it was empty, and burped.

"I'm sure you guys will cope," he smiled, pointing at Grey's bag of croissants. "You eating that?"

Grey tossed the bag at his direction and John caught it in mid-air. "I think I just lost my appetite," he said as John was already tearing through the buttery pastry.

"What's the plan, chief?" John asked with a mouthful.

"We need to lay low today. I want to run by you some basic surveillance and useful cloak and dagger techniques that may come in handy. I realize you're not going to be Jason Bourne overnight, but you're a smart kid, there's no reason for you to be an easy target."

It sounded like an insult, though John was apathetic. He finished his coffee. "Then what?" he shrugged while asking, the colour slowly returning to his face.

"On Sunday we're going to break into Babylon-on-Thames."

John's eyebrows shot up.

"If you're as good as you claim, we'll put your skills to the test when you help me find the information I need on a certain individual's computer."

"You do know they can throw me out of this country – or worst, throw me in prison." John protested but was not as edgy as yesterday, Grey noted.

"Don't worry." Grey's voice was reassuring and calm. "We're not going to get caught; besides Wey will not let anything happen to you."

John remained mute.

"Without your laptop, you will have to download the program from your company server though; we can set it up in advance later on… But are you up for it?"

John nodded.

Grey was about to turn and leave the room as John spoke. "Adam." He was hesitant. "A guy approached me last night – right there on the green."

Grey's eyes opened wide.

"He said he was with the consulate general and that he's here to help me out of this mess."

"You didn't think to mention it last night?" Grey said.

"Well, you left straight after we checked in..." John stammered. "Besides, I didn't think it was significant."

"What did you tell him?" Grey was clearly annoyed with John's naivety. There's much work yet to be done with this kid, he thought to himself, trying not to make his temper visible.

"I nearly went along, but he said something about SIS that got me thinking, how would the consulate know anything of SIS affairs. So... I pretty much told him to fuck off."

"Good lad," Grey whispered. He let out a sigh of relief. At least he was smart enough not to say anything. Well, he hoped.

"He did leave me this card with his name, Samuel Z. There's nothing else on it."

Grey's entire body went tense, his anxiety level rising again.

"You know him?" John asked.

"I've met a guy called Sammy Zcharya once. It fits."

"And?"

"Mossad. It means this runs deeper than I thought."

Grey turned around.

"Where are you going?" John protested. "I thought I was having spy camp today."

"Change of plans, kid. Since you've just now made me aware of this crucial information, I have an urgent phone call to make. We'll try to do some tutorial later and go out for dinner. Meanwhile, erm... order some room service or something... Just don't go anywhere."

Grey shot out of the room slamming the door behind him.

Chapter 20
The Telegraph

Despite the fact that it was before midday on Saturday, the *Telegraph*'s editorial board was hustling and bustling. Reporters were leaping from desk to desk, phones were ringing, and the noise of keyboards clicking was echoing above all the hubbub. Saturday was normally a busy day, as the various journalists wanted to get their pieces in the Sunday edition, which was more widely read. The *Sunday Telegraph* printing deadline was at four in the afternoon, so 'if by midday you didn't bring it home – you better go home and enjoy the rest of the weekend' was the motto of the ever reigning editor, Marcus Stein.

Katie spent the morning hours engaged in frivolous calls with her political sources. She was also trying to 'randomly' talk with colleagues, but it seemed that no one had any lead that had to do with the MoD. She was getting desperate.

The only thing close to suspicious was the fact that she could not get a hold of Jim Hogan, the *Times*' leading political correspondent. Hogan was a prick, and a hopeless drunk, but nonetheless a good reporter with sterling connections. He had a record of dozens of political sensations and was the only one ahead of Katie in the imaginary race they were having in her mind. One day she would top him and be the most senior political correspondent in the country.

She tried calling Hogan again, but he was not at his desk. The *Times* was well known for their Sunday scoops, and rumour had it that Hogan himself had stopped the press in a movie-like scene a few years back. According to the urban legend, he had taken out the main power and got into a fist fight with the unions' representative. The unions had been the main problem also in the *Telegraph*, if they had their way, the Sunday paper would be sent to press on Thursday and the weekend would start the following day. Lazy arses. Whether Hogan had actually stopped the press or whether the story was exaggerated wasn't important. The news broke just in time for the Tories' conference, and the current PM had used the scandal to overthrow his predecessor and replace him as the head of the party and the government. For Hogan to be out of the office on a Saturday so close to the issue being finalised was inconceivable. By the by, the old PM was now the Quartet's representative to the Middle East, rumoured to be the next General Secretary of the UN – another one of Jim Hogan's exclusives. Such things were news that Katie would kill in order to get first. Kill.

She decided to take the river boat from Embankment all the way to Tower Hill, where the *Times* editorial board was based. It had been years since the newspaper's editorials left Fleet Street and scattered to new, cheaper locations than the City's Square Mile. She waited for the boat to pull back to the pier, touching in with her Oyster card as soon as the drawing bridge was laid out by the boat's staff. She had been alone on the pier, and there were only a handful of people on the boat itself.

The sun that peeped out during the morning hours was already covered with a white thick cloud and the weather was gradually turning stormy. She adored the river boat ride, even through the mist; she managed to gaze at the beautiful monumental buildings such as the International Maritime Organization headquarters with its colourful mosaic of international flags; the impressive dome of St Paul's Cathedral and parallel to it, on the south bank, the Tate Modern – a brownish ghoulish building with a towering chimney. As the boat was reaching its destination, she was mesmerized by the contrast of the black glassed Shard which stood noticeably between the dreary London Bridge and the beautiful castle-like Tower Bridge. She took it all in.

***

Jim Hogan was sitting at the bar in a stuffy old drinking hole called the Big Bear. The place was nearly empty and the fake wood floor full of scratches and old spillage stains was highly visible. He was holding a half empty pint of Guinness and had an empty chaser glass standing on the bar in a small puddle of spilt scotch. He was forty-five years old and his hair was brown and unkempt. His face was droopy, as would be someone's who had already had quite a few rounds. She thought that he looked miserable.

As Katie walked in, Jim, who was acting as a self-serve barman since the other side of the bar was empty, filled the chaser all the way to the top with a Dalwhinnie single malt. As he noticed Katie he stretched all the way across the bar and salvaged another glass, filling it as well with the golden-brown liquid.

"Young Catherine, you came just in time for round three… or four… or… the truth of the matter is that I lost count…" his speech was heavy, his tongue sticking to his gums.

"It's Caitlin, you asshole." She noted that the Dalwhinnie bottle was already half empty though it wouldn't tell her exactly how much he had actually drunk from it. The only way to get Hogan to talk would be to drink with him. She just wished she'd had something to eat earlier today.

He slid the chaser glass, which halted in front of the bar stool next of him. He gestured her to sit down.

"Bottoms up," he called and they both chugged down the fifteen-year-old single malt. It tasted foul and spread a disagreeable warmth in her stomach. She wanted to throw up but fought the instinct. She was never big on scotch. The second chaser was just as bad. Olly Jones loves whisky – she played with this thought as she was choking and coughing. That seemed like the worst of it; she was starting to feel alright and already somewhat lightheaded.

"So, lass," he started, "now that you so gracefully chugged your guards away – how can I help ya?"

***

The chat with Jim was interesting. Very interesting. It took another three chasers before he started talking. Her head was spinning. He had never shared information with her in the past as he did today, presumably thanks to the influence of the alcohol. As it turned out, one of his sources in Whitewall talked about an E Squad operation that had gone bad in Chelsea. The same source had identified C on more than one occasion, attending meetings at the MoD. A different source had seen Sir Willow asking for materials in order to work on a top secret brief. The last time Sir Willow was working on something, which wasn't a fine Cognac, Thatcher had been the PM.

It also turned out that after a phone call from the owner, the *Times*' chief-editor decided there simply wasn't anything worth sending to print. The fact that Downing Street had called the owners with explicit instructions not to run a story no one had told anyone about to begin with, struck him as immensely odd. There were no 'homeland security' excuses as far as he was aware, just a blunt censorship from people too well connected.

Hogan, as drunk as he was, understood well enough what he was doing. Even when he was off the wagon he remained true to his journalistic integrity. Singing like a canary in Katie's ear was his way of overriding his spineless editor. The public has a right to know. In a sense, by pulling the plug on this story beforehand, Olly and his gang had stepped over the line. But she knew one thing: if this story was important enough to Olly to silence it, then it must be big, not the fake pretences that he tried to feed her.

She was walking to Tower Hill Tube station, resolute to get to Westminster and have a little chat with Olly Jones. She would tell him what she had found; he would have no choice but to get her *her* exclusive with the PM.

Chapter 21
Babylon-on-Thames

The cold shower that Jensen had received from C was even less agreeable than the pleasantries he had exchanged with Sammy in the morning. He sat in his office with the blinds down, smoking for the first time in days. The smoke detector was deactivated and left on the floor with its wires bulging out. With no way of cracking open the heavy glazed windows, the room was quickly full of smothering smoke.

Miss Shaw's debrief was quick and efficient. She was heading back to Grosvenor Square, with a backup team on call. Her main priority was John Daniel, and not Adam Grey. He made it clear. She was given minimal information. He gave her a new burner, but he didn't intend to stick around and see if she fished anything. This Nikolayev business must be handled by him, personally.

A sense of urgency engulfed him and sharpened his senses. He shared the opinion that the American-Iranian nuclear talks must end now, he wasn't going to let morals get in the way. Even Nelson Mandela was considered a terrorist at some point in the past, he said to himself, today his greatness admired by millions. He knew that the implications of what he was about to do were grave, but he needed the distraction. He needed the spotlight turned on terror, on the Iranians and as far as possible from the insignificant Grey and Daniel duo. He was going to stick his finger in the dam. The future depended on this.

He initiated the encryption software and started typing.

To: Marrakesh <Marrakesh _10@icloud.com>
From: sheik-davolla-salam@gmail.com

My cousin A-Salam aleikum. Please make sure our young cousin will come to his wedding on time, it should take place any day now.

The bride awaits and the dowry will be paid within the hour, via transfer-wire to your account.

    Alla be with you,

    Jamil

He hit send.

Marrakesh was the code name for a sleeper agent that had long turned into a mercenary within the North African Arab countries. Marrakesh knew how to get things done, without leaving any unwanted fingerprints. He even had ties within the unknown realm of the Islamic State, a place where most agents had turned up in an orange jumpsuit, decapitated. The service had an encyclopaedia-thick brief on Marrakesh. They had virtually every incident that had involved him the last decade.

But all this information was useless as they had not known his identity, and the fact that he was an old MI6 operative. Jensen knew his real identity; he had learned this information by sheer chance, in the process of interrogating a suspect called Sheik Davolla A-Salam back in Afghanistan in 2005. He had also learned about the Sheik's clandestine email address, used for Hezbollah-run military operations. These were generally approved by the Iranians, a perfect fake fingerprint, only back then he hadn't appreciated its full potential. Needless to mention, the subject of the interrogation did not survive. Ironically, Marrakesh, who was a zealot Muslim, knew little of the true origin of his instructions. He would have never agreed to work for a Western handler.

Marrakesh kept believing through all these years that the email was still being used by Hezbollah or some other Shiite organization, maybe the Iranian Revolutionary Guards themselves. When he assumed the account, Jensen had only identified by the name Jamil, working from Western Europe. It was easy to get Marrakesh not to ask any questions, as long as the targets remained Western and the money reached his account punctually. Marrakesh's greatest value was his close ties to some British Muslim charities. They were a known cover for Islamic terrorist operations in the UK, and were mostly under MI5 surveillance. He was sure that if this were tracked back to Marrakesh he would not have much use for this email address any more. It had already served its purpose ten times more. He minimised the encryption software and opened the mail server.

To: MI5 Liaison
CC: C, Jensen – ALL

Subject: Routine A-T Surveillance inclusions

Please include any Daawa or Charity associated with code name Marrakesh in enhanced routine surveillance.

Please include, but don't limit to, the following: El-Ichwan, FAGER, Young Muslims.

Assume there are more to include that we do not currently monitor.

Authorization code J-1-5-0-7-8-1

    Execute immediately,

JJ

He looked at the email he had just typed, deleted the word 'immediately' and replaced it with 'asap'. There. His hands are clean. 'Ish'. The problem would be that MI5 would probably only initiate the surveillance act on the following workday unless he makes some urgent calls, thus would mean that the enhanced surveillance would only initiate on Monday at some point. Regretfully, this would be too late and Marrakesh would have already acted. He lit up another cigarette and hit send.

Chapter 22
The Shard

The thirty-second floor of the Shard building, near London Bridge, was buzzing. As soon as the gorgeous hostess wearing a black cocktail dress guided them through the long dark corridor, John felt out of place in his jeans and dark sweater, which covered a plain white dress shirt. He was thankful to Grey who made him change the trainers he initially wore to elegant shoes which he brought him. How on earth did he know his shoe size? He came to realize that he needed to start paying more attention to details. Grey on the other hand was dressed immaculately, in a dark grey suit, a pink dress shirt with cufflinks and a light pink handkerchief to match, folded to two symmetrical peaks. He envied the older man's style.

The bar area was just a tad more illuminated than the dark corridor, and was infested with chatty night dwellers. Surveillance, Grey had earlier explained, is the art of blending in. He thought that he had recognized their shadow, a tradecraft's way of describing one's follower, but wasn't entirely sure. He would flush her out here, especially if she was not familiar with the square bracket shape of this restaurant and bar.

The London view was breathtaking. He had spotted all the iconic buildings, and was having problems thinking of anything else.

"Focus, lad." Grey had woken him up from his trance. "Anyone can be your shadow, though unless you had a predetermined itinerary, you can pretty much count on the fact that he will walk in to a place after you."

The background music was contemporary overly loud dance pop, and John found it hard to follow the conversation. He was at a loss. At least a dozen people had walked through the entrance to the bar, including people that went back and forth to the toilets. How could one possibly know? He turned and looked at Grey perplexed. "At least a dozen people walked through this entrance since we got here," he said.

"Eleven precisely." Grey was as sure as hell.

"Oh?"

"Three boys from the table at the end, they were taking turns going to the loo; those two blondes sitting here next to us, even you couldn't miss—" he caught their eyes and smiled at them and they giggled and started whispering, "—this bald guy who joined the table behind me, and a girl from his table that went to the toilet upon his arrival and has just returned; the couple that sat over there before and just left," he motioned with his head, "she was Indian and he was a fair-haired English—"

"I noticed them!" John jumped in.

"Then we can almost positively rule them out." He handed him a broad teeth smile and continued. "The ginger over there with the moustache, a bit of an eighties look, and the dark-haired fit bird sitting at the other end of the bar. Make it twelve, this guy is joining his mates at the table in front of us," he tilted his head, "he just walked in. By the way, you should really try the Wagyu beef they serve here."

John was impressed. He genuinely could only spot the couple Grey described, from all of these, maybe also the blonde girls.

"And who's you prime suspect?"

"If I had to guess?" Grey signalled the bartender with his hand.

"Yup."

"I'd put my money on the dark-haired girl."

"Oh?"

"She fits the profile and looks awfully familiar to me."

The barkeeper arrived and they both ordered a Grey-Goose vodka tonic.

They were sipping their drinks in silence, checking the surroundings; John was focused on the dark-haired girl. She was sitting alone drinking a glass of white wine, and was occasionally checking her phone. Is she waiting for a date? She's definitely trying to pass as someone who had been stood up. Seriously, he thought, who would stand her up? He turned to Grey and was about to ask, when the spymaster started talking. "She's making one basic mistake – working without a team."

"How can you be so certain?" He didn't mind being lectured, in fact as soon as he realized the older man had a proven record in his field, he found him quite fascinating.

"The problem is that without a team, you have to recur at some point."

"Recur?" John seemed puzzled.

"Let's put it this way, if she can't merge completely with everything you do at the exact moment you do it – then you're going to notice her."

He seemed even more puzzled.

"Okay," Grey started afresh while signalling the barkeeper to get them a second round. "Let's say you're walking in Oxford Street and you notice a street cleaner. And let's say you see the same guy, same street cleaner, now here, in the Shard's lobby. Would the penny drop?"

"Well yeah… I guess so."

"But this guy has no alternatives, as he has no team to support and switch places with him. So he can pass as the Shard's cleaner and you'll think ah okay peculiar coincidence, maybe the guy has a second job or something. But that's that, you can't catch him anywhere else otherwise that's not going to be a coincidence any more. That's presuming you'd notice the face of a street cleaner to begin with. *Capisce*?"

"Yeah so if I see this girl again, who by the way has not once looked at our direction since she got here, it would mean she's definitely my shadow."

"You got it." Grey smiled and stuffed a handful of wasabi bar nuts in his mouth.

This guy was good, John thought, his explanation made perfect sense.

"Now the hostess is coming to take us to our table, and we'll see if she's going to come after us to the restaurant side, or did she do her homework properly."

"If she comes after us?"

"Then she's afraid there's another exit to this place and would rather risk blowing her cover than lose us."

"And if she stays put?"

"Then I either underestimated her or she's not our girl."

Following the hostess, the duo made their way to the other side of the restaurant, and sat at a corner table with an amazing view as far as Westminster, John could make out the spikey parliament building and even Big Ben.

Liz Shaw did not follow them, she had in fact left the bar area soon after. She would catch them again near the hotel. The Wagyu beef was excellent.

BOOK II
Chapter 23
Manfred

Manfred Wilson didn't care about the events that had taken place the day before yesterday at Liverpool Street station. He descended the stairs from the west side of the station, as he did every morning, at 6:40 am sharp. He went past the big vertical trapeze shaped metal statue, it had a rusty brown colour, and he had never bothered to think about it or even to consider it to be a work of art. He entered the station building, glancing abruptly at the high solarium-like glass ceiling, and cruised past the doughnut, cellular phones and greeting cards glass-cube shops. He stopped his vigorous walk in front of a closed storefront, which had a white sign with 'CHEESE' on top of it, decorated with a yellow doodle of a triangular piece of Cheddar. With a rattling sound that echoed through the empty space, he took out a big set of keys and unlocked the heavy lock, he then lifted the wide sliding iron screen and opened the shop.

'CHEESE' or 'International Cheese House' as the smaller print read, was his family business, owned by his father since the fifties when it was still a small storage room on Bishopsgate Street. When the station was renovated in 1985, his dad (as did most local business owners) exercised an option to rent a shop space inside the huge station, for a relatively small annual fee and a very long lease. His father, half French from his mother's side, took advantage of some connections he had with French relatives to import rare French cheeses that nobody had even heard of in London back then. This was prior to the establishment of the European Economic Community and the little shop was a success. The good years lasted only until the mid-nineties, when European produce, especially French, became common in every supermarket in Britain, due to the, then newly formed, EU's eradication of customs for member countries. These were the years in which his father's heart condition became worse, and Manfred had taken over at the helm of the family business.

The first years were difficult, and it always seemed like his cousins, each had a small stake in the business from inheritance, were waiting for him to fail. Manfred was always branded the family's black sheep – failing in school, ruining his first marriage and getting sacked from his first and second jobs, in an ill-fated career in finance. He was constantly mocked by his relatives and the general view within the family was that eventually he would fail with the shop as well. However, he exceeded everyone's expectations and kept the boat afloat, whilst actually managing to generate small profits. Three years later his dad died from a massive heart attack (an obvious outcome of tasting his own merchandise throughout the years) and he was more determined than ever to keep the business running, on his own merit.

The economic boom of the 2000s was kind to the 'International Cheese House' and Manfred. As Liverpool Street station and its surrounding businesses grew, so did the store's profits, a direct outcome of neighbouring bankers who wanted to look sophisticated for their 'cheese and wine evenings'. It was in 2007 that everything changed: encouraged by recent profits and a second prospering marriage to a girl called Munira, he decided to expand the business and open more shops. Then it started pouring…

Everything that could have gone wrong did; a north London fraudulent property entrepreneur, a costly building integrity renovation for the station's shop and the economic crisis that hit the financial market had made people tighten their belts, literally. Manfred, whose thin blond hair dwindled considerably into a little grey fuzz, was left with debts of hundreds of thousands of pounds, and just the original shop. The cousins who had invested in the new venture saw their fortunes go down the tubes and severed any contact with him. To top it all, Munira, who had come from a Muslim home but was always secular herself, coped with things by reconnecting with her heritage, and became a devout practitioner of Islam. Their relationship had hit a dead end and Manfred truly felt alone.

A few years later, things started to look a bit less grim. He had heard back from Munira in 2011, when she needed official divorce papers signed. She was living in a communal house for divorced Muslim women, which had been sponsored by the Whitechapel Mosque. Initially the Imam dismissed her need for an official divorce process since they were married in a civil ceremony, but when she found a young new groom, the State required a bureaucratic conclusion to her prior marriage. He agreed, he didn't have any fight left in him, and after three years of not hearing from his estranged wife, he didn't really care any more.

It was Munira who then suggested that Manfred appeal to the 'Fund for Assistance and General Economic Rehabilitation' – FAGER. The word in Arabic meant 'dawn'. This was a charity organization, she explained, that looked at requests made also by 'infidel' small business owners, in return for the business keeping halal for Muslim clientele sakes.

So he applied, and aid was soon to be approved. The ham and cheese sandwiches had to go, and he agreed to keep the stock halal approved. Two hundred and fifty thousand pounds, no interest (as Islam forbids it), subject to occasional FAGER representatives' inspections. God... no – Allah bless Munira for being resourceful.

But the honeymoon with FAGER lasted exactly a hundred days, after which a representative named Hani paid the shop a visit. Hani had a small, well-trimmed beard, a black suit with white pinstripes, and Manfred couldn't help staring at his spikey hair and curved sideburns. He explained that the contract Manfred had signed gave the Fund entitlement to collect occasional logistic favours from the aided business. Manfred who had been all too keen to get the quarter million pounds and didn't bother with the fine print was enraged, but Hani remained calm and requested nothing tangible for the time being.

He sought legal counsel after that visit, but the terms of the loan, which were more than indulging, stated clearly that failure to comply with any reasonable demand could result with an immediate loan recall. Thus Manfred was forced to adopt an ostrich policy, burying his head in the sand and gritting his teeth whenever the Fund came with one of its peculiar requests.

At first the 'logistic favours' were fairly small: providing free sandwiches for a Muslim school fieldtrip, arranging a tour of the East End for Muslim women (equipped with an

Arab translator), and similar tasks. It was only in the past two years that the favours became more and more erratic, the latest he would describe as highly unusual.

The call arrived a week ago, after months in which the Fund had been silent, and Manfred even thought (more hoped) that they had forgotten about him. He was balancing his books and looked at the annual loan statement. The account was still in debt in excess of two hundred thousand pounds, and due to the store's disappointing quarter, he seriously considered calling for an extended loan – an emergency clause that calls for additional funds to any business facing insolvency. This was a quick process that would result in the money being in the bank within a week. The temptation was high, but Manfred's conscience didn't let him proceed with the online application form. It was obvious that the funding source was highly shady and the implications of tightening the already strangling knot with FAGER could be perilous.

As he was weighing his options the landline in his flat rang. Nobody had used this number for years. His anxiety level was rising.

"Hullo," he said the word quietly, nearly choking from the saliva that accumulated in his throat. Beads of sweat were forming on his temples.

"Mr Wilson?" a voice said with a Levantine accent that would most definitely have exposed a smile full of teeth.

Manfred remained silent.

"Manfred, are you there?" The tone had changed and the gentleman on the other end of the line seemed irritated.

"Yeah, yeah," he stammered. "What is it this time?"

He was spot on, it was yet another favour. The man on the other end of the line was called Hamoodi, an affectious shortening of the name Mohamed, though he didn't feel much affection for the guy at this exact moment. The request was elaborated: Manfred was to be alone in the shop around closing time the next evening, somewhere before 6 pm a package would be delivered. This package was to be held for a special guest who may choose to stay overnight at the shop. Manfred was to attend to the guy's every needs.

"What's in the package?" he asked suspiciously.

"Nothing interesting," Hamoodi assured, and added, "Logistics."

The line clicked, or did Hamoodi deliberately ring off? He was pondering as to the disappearance of Mr Hani, maybe a dismissal on grounds of excessive hair gel usage? He tried not to think about the package as he went into the kitchen to heat up his ready-made dinner.

Chapter 24
Ahmed

Ahmed A-Salam's early childhood in the West Bank was a good one. He was born and raised in Jericho, in the early nineties, a time when the area saw an economic boost after the Oslo peace process had started, and the Israeli-Palestinian conflict looked like it was drawing to an end. The newly built casino in Jericho brought jobs and prosperity to the residents, and even his street in Aqabat Jaber refugee camp, started to look more and more like one of Jericho's suburban neighbourhoods, when proper brick buildings had been erected. His father found a job in accounting in the casino, and his mother worked as a teacher, for one of Fatah's secular nurseries, sponsored by the newly formed Palestinian Authority. Routinal 'normal' life, one which his parents never knew, was kind to Ahmed, he was a straight-A student and very popular among his school friends. He had two sisters: Saima who had just started preschool, and Khadija a six-month-old baby who was enrolled in the Hamas-run nursery, the only nursery actually inside the refugee camp.

It all changed in the year 2000, right after Ahmed's thirteenth birthday. This was the year when the boy Ahmed was no longer, and his childhood had come to an abrupt end. With the collapse of the peace talks and start of *Al-Aqsa Intifada*, the second Palestinian uprising, Jericho was engulfed in flames and chaos, like many of the West Bank cities. The Israeli Defence Forces (the IDF) were forced to bombard the Jericho casino, after Palestinian forces had used the building as a base from which they fired at the Israeli soldiers. A week later, the worst had struck. It was unfortunate, was the phrase the Palestinian officials used, that just as Ahmed's mother went to pick up little Khadija, the 'Mukawama Forces' fled to the inside of the nursery after a confrontation with an IDF patrol. His mother, along with his sister, another teacher and six more infants had been caught in the crossfire, and had been killed. Hamas officials, the biggest Islamic faction, came to offer their condolences and support. They were quick to proclaim that the Zionists bullets were at fault (though they never offered an explanation as to why the brave fighters fled into a nursery and started shooting from within it). And that was it: Ahmed's father was left a widower with two kids and was unemployed now that the casino was reduced to rubble.

And yet, Hamas were good to them. Since the 'martyrdom' of his mother and sister, the aid money was paid every month. In gratitude, his father was drawn towards Islam, and became a prominent local speaker against the Israeli occupation.

Ahmed and his sister were moved to the care of his aunt and uncle in Ramallah, and were both registered to Hamas-run schools, on a full scholarship. Ahmed's hatred towards the Zionists grew stronger every year. When he started his academic studies in the University of Birzeit, he was naturally accepted as a member of the 'Kutla Islamia' – Hammas' student body. During those years, Ahmed initiated charity work of his own, and grew closer and closer to Islam. He was a scrawny youth with a dark complexion and black curly hair. Under his big brown eyes, there was always a flicker of sadness kneaded with hatred.

This hatred along with the desire to avenge his mother's and sister's deaths drove him. It was feeding and intensifying from his surroundings on a daily basis: the Imam who kept referring to Ahmed as 'the Shahida's little boy'; the *mudir* in the *Daawa* branch who kept cursing the Jews whether they were at a fund-raiser or handing out food packets to the poor; his infrequent visits to his father, who became a Muslim zealot and abandoned the Western way of life completely; and even the women of El-Ram (the high-end neighbourhood of Ramallah), who were full of admiration to the brave martyrs and promised Ahmed a good wife, if he remained a devoted Muslim. Ironically, the thought of prearranged marriage appealed to him the most, as he was rather shy when it came to matters of the heart. Even though he was physically small, Ahmed was determined to fight the infidels. He wanted to do something that would forever act as a memorial to his family name, to be written in the book of the heroes of the resistance. These were the Imam's exact words when he described Ahmed to the brethren from the Muslim Brotherhood who visited Ramallah the other week. The Imam's praising had worked and he managed to secure Ahmed a scholarship to spend a term studying Koran in the Luton Madrassa. Ahmed was overjoyed when he received the news, but he had bigger plans. He would not waste his innocent looking physique and the visa to Britain on trivial school studies. No! Ahmed was destined for greatness.

Chapter 25
Liverpool Street Station: Present Day

It was already 7 pm on Saturday when a metallic knock was heard on the 'International Cheese House' shop's front door. Manfred had already dozed off in a chair in a back alcove of the shop that served as an office. He was startled and woke up to answer the door. The image of the thin boy with black curly hair and round glasses overthrew him. It was not what he expected. The boy was wearing an olive green Gant polo shirt, and grey cargo trousers. He was plain looking with no distinctive features, except that he had visible sweat marks on his fuzzy moustache and underneath the armpits. It was freezing cold outside.

"Mr Wilson?" His English was carrying a Middle Eastern accent.

"Yes… yes," Manfred stammered again.

"Are you alright, sir?" His shy gaze carried some sort of politeness that was hard to find in today's youth, Manfred reflected.

"Yes, yes… I mean you have come to the right place, please come in." Manfred had opened the door and left it ajar, as they stepped into the small space.

"I believe you may have signed for a package for me?"

"Yes, it's in the back," he answered.

"I hope it is okay that I ask you to wait outside? For modesty reasons of course."

Manfred nodded. The package had arrived the day before via a courier service company that he had never heard of. A big cardboard box. He wasn't sure what to make of it, and was quite anxious. But now, something in the unremarkable boy got Manfred to ease up. His English was accurate yet archaic and mechanical. He seemed to Manfred to be utterly harmless. If the Muslim boy needed some privacy in order to change and freshen up, that was fine by him.

***

His instructions were to wait till the late morning hours. The majority of people travel late during the weekends, and going about it too early would be less rewarding, especially on a Sunday. "Patience is the key to salvation," his Imam used to say back in Ramallah.

Staying all night at the shop was not an option, in case he had been seen walking in. He had checked the contents of the box. Among other items, it contained a black wheeled trolley, which he filled with the other items. He went to a Travel Lodge located on City Road, close by. The room was tidy and clean, allowing him to spend the night in preparations and prayer.

The next day, at 11 am sharp, Ahmed entered Liverpool Street Underground station, dragging the black wheeled trolley behind him. He went down the escalator, and boarded a westbound Central Line train, headed for the West End. As he had been warned, the train was busy and stuffy, and he felt he was suffocating from the on-board heating. His anxiety and expectations also contributed to his over sweating, and he had hoped that nobody noticed the wetness of his back. He leaned tighter to the pole, in the middle of the cart. His heart was thumping and felt like it would soon leap out of his chest. He was certain that everyone in close proximity to him could hear it beating.

At Holborn station he managed to take a seat next to a little girl who was sitting across from her mother. They both had strawberry blonde hair and their resemblance was uncanny. Across from his own seat sat a black woman in her forties, her hair was entwined with colourful beads. To his left, many people were standing up, crowding the aisle of the train. He noticed two young and vocal Spanish Mochilas, a few groups of tourists, and could even spot an old Muslim, dressed in a tradition Gallabiyah. He will be a *Shahid Be-Iden, Allah.* A martyr, God willing, he thought to himself.

His fear intensified and his mouth went dry. He brushed his hair with his palm, and it felt entirely wet. He mumbled the Shahada, the Muslim testimony, a trick the Imam had taught him to gain courage. As he sank into deep thoughts about his family, his mother and his infant sister that never got the chance to grow up, his eyes filled with tears, and his hatred intensified within him. He looked right only to see the little blonde girl making faces at him. His lips opened in an awkward sort of way but he couldn't mutter a sound, he instead formed a wide genuine smile. "Allah is merciful towards the innocents," his Imam had said. At that exact moment he heard the combination of words he was eager to hear: "This is Oxford Circus." There was a chime, and the train doors started to open, he reached deep into his pocket and pulled hard on the switch.

Chapter 26
The West End

The noise was deafening. Then a remote humming. Exposed electricity noise. Sparks.

The smoke mushroom was clearly apparent above Oxford Circus, seconds after the charge went off. Screams were heard from every direction. The sirens were already screeching from afar. The British were good at first response ever since World War II and through the years of IRA terror, but only minutes later when the thick smoke started to fade, could the rescue services enter the station. Another fear was from the risk of second and third charges that would imitate the multi-epicentre attack of 7/7, the 7th July Tube attacks back in 2005.

The officers who went in first identified the magnitude of the destruction: dark soot covered the station walls, bodies were scattered everywhere. There were a few neon lights that were flickering on and off, but it was the first responders' torches that illuminated the area, and aided in the discovery of a few living but injured survivors.

Later it would be learned that the charge was a military issued one, attached to a makeshift detonator. The assailant's timing was sadly perfect: he delivered the deadly blow as soon as the doors started opening, and in this split second the shock wave managed to reach as many people as possible, both on board and on the platform. This same shock wave had in effect crushed the bodies of the commuters, and did not skip even those who were second and third in line to board the train. Whoever was in close proximity to the charge stood no chance.

Evacuating the survivors was a wretched task, as the magnitude of the catastrophic event was slowly uncovered. Injured commuters started surfacing from both Tottenham Court Road and Bond Street stations, most of the people suffered from shock, and commuters who had stood in the other stations, even far from the epicentre, were injured from debris and wreckage.

***

Adam Grey woke up in complete darkness. Sounds of exposed electricity cables bursting and echoing shrieks were the first sounds he could make out through the ringing sound in his ears. The concrete floor felt warm under his back, and his body felt like it had been hit by a truck. He gathered his bearings and using his right arm, which was quite numb, started feeling his torso, looking for open wounds. Everything seemed in place, yet a puddle of blood drenched his clothes. He concluded that the blood could have been someone else's, he was lying next to a few people, most likely bodies, as they were still, like overturned statues.

The feeling slowly came back to his arm and a sharp thumping headache attacked him. As his eyes became used to the darkness, he could make out a few bodies around him. He tried lifting himself but failed, it seemed that his legs were trapped under a heavy metal pipe.

He had left the Millennium Mayfair that morning, John still asleep in his own room. He stopped for a cup of coffee from the deli in Mount Street. He was supposed to meet up with Wey, and that was all he could remember. He must have boarded the Central Line, aiming to change for the Victoria Line towards the SIS building. He wasn't sure. He couldn't remember the train or the blast. One second he was paying for coffee, and the next he woke up here. He was looking for his mobile phone but it was nowhere to be found. He heard voices and could make out spots of light in the distance. He attempted to shout but his vocal cords could only produce a faint sigh. When he tried again he felt as if he was drowning in his own saliva. He closed his eyes and waited in the dark.

***

Matt Wey had arrived at Piccadilly Circus and been immediately stopped by the police that blocked the street. Even his SIS badge didn't help. "Apologies, sir, but the vehicle stays here," said the ranking sergeant at the roadblock who was under strict instructions to keep the roads in the contained perimeter clear. Wey cursed but left the car on the kerb in Piccadilly Street, with a flashing police light apparent on the dashboard. He started running up towards Oxford Circus.

As soon as Grey was late to their meeting, scheduled at the Tate Britain, Wey knew that something was wrong. He tried Grey's mobile a few times and reached the voicemail immediately. As he ran back to Vauxhall Cross he rang operations and asked them to see if they could locate Mr Suarez in the hotel's vicinity. The answer was negative. Then the reports started coming in.

Amidst the chaos that held the Oxford Circus area, Wey tried to find Grey. He was randomly searching between the injured that were being hauled into the fleet of ambulances already parked around the crossroads, but knew that finding him would be nearly impossible. There was no way of using the service or their link would be exposed, an unwanted outcome in case that Grey was alive and well. He was standing helpless in front of the big Top Shop store and tried to arrange his thoughts. They were on the final lap and they just lost their front runner. He must find the young foreigner. In a sharp motion he untied the knot of his tie and stuffed it in his jacket pocket. He turned left and started running like a maniac towards Mayfair.

***

John recognized her among the crowd that started accumulating near Hanover Square, which was closed towards both Oxford and Regent Streets' directions. During his time in the city, he had never experienced a greyer and more bewildered London. The sun shone on the blazing hot incident area, adding insult to injury.

It was only yesterday night that Grey thought he had made her, and there she was, despite everything still acting as a shadow as sure as eggs were eggs. She was standing between the people, constantly checking her mobile phone.

"Hey!" he called. "You! Stop!" he hollered and nobody took notice.

He made me, Liz thought to herself. As soon as she heard the blast she tried contacting Jensen, then Ops, but it seemed as if the entire network had collapsed. She had seen Adam Grey walking towards Bond Street in the morning and she was worried about him. She had been refused entrance to the Oxford Circus area despite her badge. "It's too dangerous, ma'am," the sergeant who was twenty years her elder had said. "The book says we must wait in case there's a second blast. Except the first responders, nobody is getting in there." She had no choice but to wait.

She remained waiting by the police barrier even as the crowd thinned. And now he made her. A rooky mistake. Would she deny? Would she admit and the hell with the operation? He drew near.

"I need your help!" He was panting.

She remained speechless.

"Adam Grey. He's missing."

She opened a pair of calf-like eyes, yet remained mute.

John grabbed her by the shoulders and started shaking her. "Snap out of it! It's not the time to play spies." His English was fluent, far more than what she had assumed. "I think he was on the Tube – you must help me find him!"

She started stammering but in her heart knew that he was right. She must help Adam Grey. It's not the time to play games, someone just detonated a bomb on her country's soil. "Let's go – I know a way that may still be open," she said. They both doubled back and started running towards Bond Street.

Chapter 27
Whitehall

The phone lines in Olly Jones' office wouldn't stop ringing. The PM's office had announced a press conference scheduled for 2 pm, but it would probably only take place sometime during the evening hours. Downing Street was in turmoil, the ambiance set heavy on the small room adjoining the PM's office. In a meeting that included Sir Willow, the Permanent Under-Secretary for Defence, the personal aide to the Home Secretary (who was too occupied to attend herself) and the heads of SIS, MI5 and GCHQ, everyone had to admit that they didn't have a single lead. When the majority of the participants had left, Sir Willow, Stamper and Olly remained on their own.

"Tell me, Tony," Olly started, "that we didn't have any initial knowledge of this shit before I send the Prime Minister to face a press conference lynching."

Now that most participants had left, Sir Willow allowed himself to set free a silver flask that was kept in his suit's inner pocket.

"Terrible… Terrible…" mumbled Sir Willow and took a large swig from the flask.

Olly was quick to connect the dots: in the earlier meeting, the head of MI5 mentioned a surveillance order that was received the day before from Jamie Jensen, the head of the small Counterintelligence Department of MI6. He even offered they'd summon Jensen, a suggestion that was immediately rejected by Stamper. He was genuinely surprised by the surveillance order, having neglected to check his email this weekend.

Stamper advocated that the order was sent by one of Jensen's men, as a result of budget cuts in MI6, which currently had no excess funds for extended counterintelligence activity. He said it with such conviction, that he even shot a dirty look towards Sir Willow, whose ministry controls the intelligence services' budgets through the JIC. Well played, Stamper, Olly conceded at that moment.

"I can't guarantee anything at this point!" Stamper was practically crying. "It's hard to imagine that anyone within our ranks would even fathom to do anything other but to stop an event like this. Nonetheless, it seems that Jensen had intel of some sort and was busy covering his own arse while neglecting to sound the alarm… Okay?" He was edgy and stroppy.

"Did you talk to Jensen?"

"He's… He's unavailable," he stammered.

"What do you mean? Where the hell can the head of your counterintelligence department be at a time like this?!" Olly's impatience turned into fury.

"He's on a plane."

Both men's eyebrows rose in astonishment.

"He had cleared it with me," he sounded insincere. "I told him to take care of the Iranian mess first-hand."

"Where is he?" Sir Willow asked slowly.

"You don't need to know, sir, with all due respect." Stamper glanced at him from the side of his shoulder.

"So he's in Iran," Olly half-asked, he couldn't hide his annoyance. He didn't try to.

"Not sure, the Professor wasn't spotted arriving there as we planned. That's why Jensen is off now." He loosened his double Windsor knot and swallowed hard.

"Let me make some sense from it all," Olly was steaming. "With the passport we helped him get, the nuclear scientist went AWOL?"

Meanwhile, Sir Willow, whose face was already quite red, emptied the flask with another big swig.

"Yes that is correct," Stamper said apathetically.

That was the moment that Olly decided that enough time had already been wasted. He said his goodbyes and headed back to his office in Whitehall.

***

If there was only one thing that Olly Jones had learnt in politics, it was that every event – whether positive or not – had a winner and a loser. There was never just one player, it was always a zero sum game. In the aftermath, if someone was standing in front of the cameras grinning, there was equally someone who was at home planning his retirement. This winner would not necessarily be the one who had done particularly well, but the guy who simply managed to 'spin' things his way.

He had numerous examples for this; his most prominent one was when as Secretary of State for Energy, the current

PM had cut a ribbon inaugurating a new nuclear power plant in the greater Glasgow area. The plant helped create hundreds of new jobs in the area, and the Secretary took full credit at the grand opening. It wasn't an easy task spinning it so that the Secretary could reap the praises, as he had advocated for years against nuclear power and its implementation. But luckily public opinion was shaped using people's short term memory, and while the Tories claimed credit, the Glasgow plant was actually an outcome of a persistent lobbying by a Labour backbencher. That MP's misfortune was that he had lost his parliamentary seat only weeks before the plant had finally opened. The State Secretary for Energy was luckily just appointed in time, in order to swoop in on the prize. That ex MP was, to the best of his knowledge, working nowadays as a schoolmaster somewhere near Aberdeen…

Olly Jones was genuinely worried; this was turning from a mere policy cock-up to a genuine nightmare. He was adamant: this time he comes first, the PM second and the rest of the rats can go down with the ship. He hit the intercom buzzer quite firmly. "Trish!" he yelled to his PA as if she were miles away. "Get me Katie Jones, tell her to be here on the double." Before she even acknowledged him he added, "Tell her she has an exclusive with… Oliver Jones.

Chapter 28
Euston Square

University College of London Hospital (UCH) was starting to calm down from what had been a very hectic day. Ambulances had evacuated the majority of the wounded to its A & E. The police had closed the streets leading from Oxford Circus to the hospital, thus allowing a quick evacuation route. Around 1 pm the hospital's general director had announced that they could no longer support the admission of any new patients, and non-urgent cases had been referred to more distant hospitals.

Adam Grey's wounds were not as acute as the medical team had initially assessed. About two hours after he was found and treated, it was apparent that none of his internal injuries would require an emergency operation and he was left to rest in the Internal Medicine ward with round the clock monitoring. He had a fractured collar bone and sustained bone fractures in both legs. His short term memory was compromised as well: he still had no recollection between buying coffee and waking up after the blast. When he regained consciousness he had an acute migraine, which grew strong and unbearable when he had strained his mind to try and remember more.

It was Wey who had finally spotted him on one of the stretchers, and insisted upon his immediate evacuation. He had arranged for Grey to have a room to himself, and had ordered the staff to call his mobile as soon as Grey regained consciousness.

John slammed shut the window of the minimal grey-white hospital room. "This ambulance noise is driving me crazy! I have no idea how you managed to sleep." He smiled.

"Try being in a train wreck," Grey muttered, struggling with the words. "Besides, I have no idea what they've been feeding me here, but I feel sleepy." He sighed.

Liz sat in the corner of the room. It was clear that her initial mission was over, but she could not reach Jensen or get any straight order from Ops. The service was in utter chaos, it took three tries to get the officer on duty, and he was of little or no help at all. They had met Matt Wey as they managed to reach Oxford Street station, and this encounter had reshuffled the deck. He immediately issued an interim directive annexing her to his department. Her mission had changed, it was now to protect and monitor Adam Grey. A babysitting assignment, at a time like this. And again Adam Grey.

While sitting on the small hospital chair her phone chimed and she could see the official operation order, annexing her to the Internal Comptroller Department. She must report directly to Neil Finch, one of the veteran operations officers she had vaguely known.

"What is she doing here?" Grey suddenly asked turning his attention to Liz.

"It's alright." John calmed him down. "Matt officially added her to our team. She knew nothing; she wasn't a part of it."

Grey managed a nod.

Their team?! Was the young Mr Daniel a part of the service now? She wondered. Could this impertinent guy be in on things that were kept secret from her?!

"I think it's about time you filled me in," she finally said with an authoritarian voice. "Especially if you expect me to help."

Chapter 29
Whitehall

Olly's room was as dreary as ever. He stood up and tilted the shades so that the late afternoon light could wash over the small office space. Opposite his big desk sat Katie Jones. The gorge between them was far greater than the width of the desk.

"So the reason I got you here was to try and clarify some of the things l may have implied when we… erm… when we last—"

"Cut the crap, Olly!" she threw out. "First you send me on a wild goose chase, then you decide to come clean, yesterday your assistant nearly had security remove me from the premises… which is it?" She was genuinely furious.

He tried to talk but she went on.

"Just to have you know, I did some digging and I found out that you pulled the plug on a piece that the *Times* was going to run today, care to explain, huh?" He couldn't get a word in. "So now let's hear why. Why is Sir Willow buzzing behind the scenes and doing his own leg work? What have you done?" She caught her breath and gritted her teeth. The steam now set loose.

"Before I tell you, you must promise to protect me—"

"I promise you nothing, Olly – one way or another I'll get the story, with or without your help." She was like a teenager waking up from a silly crush.

"Listen to me!" It was his turn. "A lot is riding on what you may or may not write. And you will get your exclusive, and this will be the biggest thing you ever did."

"But?"

"But. But you need to protect me, if not for my sake then for our future. Nobody else is going snatch it from beneath your nose, but the next twenty-four hours are crucial, and yes if I can still pull a nuke-free Middle East… Let's just say that I would give a lot to make it happen."

"Nukes? What does that have to do with anything? What else would you do to achieve your ambitions, Olly? Would you have our freedom revoked? The freedom of the press?"

"In a heartbeat," he said with assurance yet his look was evasive.

She thought hard for a few seconds, and stared into his eyes. He seemed sincere, and she would need his help. Having him on record would be solid gold. "Okay, Olly Jones. You get your twenty-four hours. When do I interview you?"

"That won't be necessary." He opened the desk drawer and took out a disk-on-key. He threw it on the wide desk towards her.

"What's this?" She tilted her head towards the device.

"My brief."

"What prevents me from running this tomorrow?" She reached out and grabbed it, pocketing the device in one swift motion.

"Password protected. You'll get the code tomorrow."

She sighed out loud. She could try, but it would probably be close to impossible to break the code in time. Besides, she gave him her word.

"Tell me one thing, Olly."

"Shoot."

"Do we know who's behind the attack this morning?"

He remained silent.

She gave him a minute then broke the silence. "Well?!"

"I certainly hope not."

"What is that supposed to mean?" She could not help but show her frustration with the ambiguous answer.

"It means that I can make a good guess"

"And what if you're right?"

"Off the record?"

She nodded.

"Then God have mercy on us all."

Chapter 30
Thirty miles North-East of Ar-Raqqah, Syria

The Yak-40 Jet had come to a halt on the sandy runway. It was the landing from hell – bumpy and terrifying with the wind whipping the old Russian jet ferociously, swinging it from side to side like a marionette on strings. Jamie Jensen reflected on the last memorable twenty minutes in which the plane battled the elements and landed successfully. He remained in his tan leather seat while the engines started to cool down. The pilot and co-pilot got out of the cockpit and opened the hatch door. Both had Arabic features: dark complexion, black hair, and they both wore thick moustaches topped with eighties style Ray-Bans.

"What now?" Jensen sprayed towards them, but the pair ignored the venomous outburst and stepped out of the plane without even a word. The co-pilot managed a glance towards Jensen that he read as 'you can climb down or drop dead for all I care', and shot off. The jet had been in the air for over two hours, and Jensen was tired. He managed to take a night flight from London to Beirut. There, the blue painted Yak-40 was waiting for him in a private hangar in the Rafic Hariri Airport, dwarfing the other executive jets in size, but lacking style and looking obsolete.

He gathered his hand luggage, straightened his white cotton shirt, and climbed down the ladder onto the sandy surface. The wind blew stronger, and grains of sand got into his eyes, leaving an irritating sensation and making him tearful. He took out a pair of mirrored Oakley sunglasses that were more suitable for a teenager, and lit up a cigarette, staring into the horizon.

The sand dunes seemed endless; the sun was just starting its descent towards the western skyline, still striking hot in full throttle. He was already sweating in his English cut woollen trousers. The wind grew even stronger and the sand dunes, almost white, seemed to be shifting behind the heat shimmers. White clouds appeared on the horizon, but they did not seem to block even a single ray. Bloody desert, he thought to himself.

The jet was supposed to take him to an unknown location where he would meet Nikolayev in the flesh and discuss how to proceed. He was well aware that he instigated an awful thing back home, and that London would be in chaos by now, with armed police patrolling the streets and endless deliberations in the House of Commons, demanding somebody's head on a pike. He was fairly sure that his involvement was left unknown, and he would still be able to talk his way out of whatever inquiry that came his way. Nevertheless, the distraction was essential for the plan to follow through, and for the Americans to stay out of the nuclear talks and pushed towards renewed sanctions over Iran. Sadly the British no longer had real teeth when it came to leading Western policy. Therefore events must be moulded. He had no remorse.

He took out his mobile phone. He had tried to remain off the grid so far, but desperate times call for desperate measures, and he was not entirely sure where he was. He figured out that the plane either landed in some deserted area north or north-east of Beirut, judging by the sun's location in the course of their flight. He hoped it was the former and that they were in Turkey.

He could see a small dust cloud low on the horizon, but he didn't bother thinking about it, as he was waiting for his phone to find a network. Nada. Where did those insolent pilots disappear to? He started wondering. He wasn't worried that he was left out to rot, as he was fairly sure that no one would desert a jet worth millions of dollars without claiming it and flying it back to civilization at some point. So he figured that as long as he stayed put, nothing bad would be inflicted upon him. Still, the fact that the phone found no signal was disturbing.

As he lifted his gaze, visibly sweating now, he could see that the dust cloud drew near. In fact, it resembled a miniature tornado – twirling, pushing grey sand particles and growing in size with every passing second. From the horizon he could make out two shapes amid the dust, but it took at least three more minutes of squinting into the retina-burning sand until he realized that these were two figures on horseback, making their way towards him. As the scene unravelled, it appeared that the horses' charge was the source of the mini storm, and as they reached a shooting distance, he could no longer distinguish the dust twirl and the horizon. He could taste the foul sand in his mouth.

The two horsemen halted their stampede about five metres from the plane. They were both wearing dark cargo trousers and olive-coloured army style shirts, only partly visible as they had black kufiyahs and shawls draping their bodies. The horses were of big Arabian breed, their colour blackish brown, and seemed unaffected by the weight of their saddles that were loaded with huge dusty kitbags. The rider on the left had a visible AK-47 slung over his shoulder in some sort of satchel, but he was in no rush to un-holster it.

"Comrade Jensen!" the unarmed horseman called out with a Russian accent.

He thought he recognized the voice, but it had been a while now. Still, could he be that daft, after all he risked for him, to drag him to this… this hellhole? Jensen refused to believe. He didn't even know where they were. And where were the damn pilots? He'd had enough of this ordeal, and started walking back towards the plane's ladder.

"JAMIE JENSEN!" the guy yelled and dismounted in a quick leap.

Jensen halted and turned to the source of the sound, as the man walked rapidly towards him. The other figure stayed on his horse, controlling it to move in small strides in place and prevented it from straying after his peer. The dismounted man reached a spitting distance from Jensen and started unwrapping his black head wear. A dishevelled Professor Nikolayev was revealed, his skin tone was darker than Jensen remembered, and his beard grew long and grey. He smelled like he could use a shower, Jensen thought.

"Are you out of your fucking mind?!" Jensen shouted, then eased down his voice. "What am I doing here? Where is here anyway?"

"We are in Syria," Nikolayev commented with no apparent expression. "Not far from Ar-Raqqah. Capital of the Caliphate, or at least some of it… Beautiful place," he chuckled.

"You are mad!" Jensen said, as if proclaiming a well-known fact. "You know what will happen if the Islamists hear that you are around? They will make every effort to capture you. Are you riding with the rebels?" Jensen gestured towards the armed horseman. "Do they guarantee our safety in this godforsaken place?" He had an image of himself wearing the notorious orange jumpsuit and his head paraded unattached to his body, in some sort of video for the infidels to see. He did not care to be in this place and he was going to do everything in his power to get the Russian plane back in the air asap.

"The jihadists are exactly what we are looking for, Jamie." He used his Christian name.

"We?" Jensen protested. "I didn't ask to be here, in fact, I insist that you call back your sorry excuse of a pilot and let me fly away from this mess."

He ignored the pleading. "*We*, is exactly right. Have you seriously thought I would not figure out your little plans? Get me in Teheran, get the West to walk away from the already concluded nuclear disarmament deal, and then get rid of me before they could actually connect the dots and realize that the Iranians had nothing to do with this. *N'est pas?*"

Jensen remained silent. This was unexpected. If Nikolayev truly went back on their deal and only used him to get to the Islamic realm, then there was no telling what might happen next. Was he crazy enough to make a dirty bomb for them? Well, he was certainly greedy enough to put the world on a brink of mutual assured destruction in the past.

"This is crazy," Jensen said.

"Enlighten me," Nikolayev snorted in contempt.

"You cannot control these people. It's not like dealing with the Russians or even the North Koreans. When they learn of your whereabouts, they will come for you. And you will be doomed either way. Now there's still time to get the hell out of here and back to Teheran or Dubai or anywhere you want to. For fuck's sake, I'll even drink mojitos with you in Cabo if you step down from your high horse and call this off; whatever this is!"

Nikolayev had never seen Jamie Jensen so frightened. But this was irrelevant. He was fairly sure he could drag the Islamists by their ears, and manage the best of both worlds. He was promised a title of an Emir, with all the benefits he could dream of. Heck, it was better than living in some dump in Brazil for the rest of his days. But he needed Jensen. The chaos that roamed in London wasn't enough, it would buy him time and leave him insignificant in the eyes of the Western intelligence services for now. By the time the world turned its attention back to the conclusion of the nuclear talks, he would have long concluded a deal with the Islamists. Jensen was his ace up the sleeve, in case things took a turn to the worse. He made a signal to his rebel chaperone using his index finger. These guys were so loyal and overprotective; you just had to provide them with a few weapons in their fight against the Syrian regime.

The horse started creeping slowly towards Jensen, in small strides. Jensen, all too aware of his predicament, turned to Nikolayev. "Okay, you got it your way. You managed to play me, what could you possibly want from me now?" he demanded.

"My dear Jamie. Haven't you realized already? You are my get out of jail free card!" Nikolayev laughed. And with a quick long stride, his jihadi companion's steed charged towards Jensen. It took less than five seconds for the stallion to reach Jensen, and the face-covered Arab unsheathed the Kalashnikov in a swift motion, and struck him on the head with its butt. Jensen fell unconscious; like a rag doll.

"Saddle him up, Omar!" Nikolayev commanded. "We have a long way still to ride today." He had mounted his horse and they started riding towards the sun.

Chapter 31
Euston Square

It was six thirty in the evening. The events of the day seemed like ancient history, though the special afternoon news bulletins were running the same images over and over again. The ward was relatively quiet. Liz was still sitting on the same corner chair, overlooking Adam Grey, who was asleep. John had returned to the hotel about an hour earlier when the Sister had asked them to leave. Liz had insisted she was Grey's daughter, and was reluctantly allowed to stay outside of visiting hours.

The ridiculous claim that someone within the service was in bed with a former KGB officer had enraged her. The explanations John provided were circumstantial at best. She wished Grey was up and running so she could confront him with this lunacy. There was no point taking it up with Wey, he was like a dog with a bone, anxious to dig up any dirt he could. She dismissed John's so-called proofs one by one. Some guys shooting at him around Chelsea was maybe excessive, but it didn't prove that something inside the service was corrupt. They dared implicate C as well, the nerve!

The Prime Minister's press conference was eventually held at 6 pm. He looked awful. He was unkempt and pale, his performance was shaky and his speech was slurred. He could not calm anyone nor provide any detail. It was a mess. Liz had deduced that either the situation was too complex to give any details in a short reports brief, or that they simply hadn't the vaguest clue who was behind the monstrous attack. Thus far no organization had claimed responsibility, whereas you'd think they'd be lined up to do so, after pulling something like this. It was mind boggling.

She was having a cup of strong tasting hospital tea, when she spotted a shadow outside the opaque glass door. The handle started turning and Liz stood up quietly, drawing her standard issue Walther.

As she crouched she knocked over some medical supplies. A loud metallic bang echoed through the room as they hit the floor, causing the shadow to halt and slowly double back. "Fuck," she muttered and sprang out to the corridor. There was no one there, but she could hear the staircase door closing with a click. She started running towards the source of the noise.

She quickly descended the neon-lit staircase and just managed to kick open a closing door leading to the ground floor. As she ran towards the hospital's exit, she caught a glimpse of the character, just running through the front doors. He was wearing a thick dark down-filled jacket and was signalling a car. "Hey! Stop that guy!" she called out to the elderly security guard, but he reacted slowly. She was already outside when the guy rode away in a grey Toyota Prius.

She started running towards the junction but before she could take a good look at the passenger, the light turned green and the Prius took a left turn. She kept running into the road, and to the sounds of screeching car wheels that nearly ran her down, turned left on Huntley Street, staying behind the car. She spotted a black taxi cab parked on the side of the street, the driver enjoying a sandwich. She climbed in the back seat, as the driver turned to her with a mouth full of food. "Look, ma'am, I'm done for the—" He stopped when he spotted the lamplight reflection bouncing from her handheld Walther.

"Follow that Uber!" she ordered, and the taxi took off.

Chapter 32
Knightsbridge

The Toyota pulled up on the left side of the road next to the Knightsbridge Underground station sign. She could see the man getting out in a hurry and going through the main doors of the behemoth of a building that was Harrods. The department store's pale yellow-orange bricks were shining brilliantly from the night lights, irritating Liz's eyes.

"Pull over here," she instructed the taxi driver, who did not dare argue. She jumped out, noticing the emptiness of the street and road, presumably due to this morning's murderous attack. She swooshed past the security guard without returning his courteous greeting and entered the bright cosmetics shopping rooms. It was white, so white! She was disoriented for a moment. She could not spot the dark coat anywhere between the white-lit cosmetics stands, so she kept straight. There were still a few tourists in the big boutique, shopping obliviously to the chaos that had taken place just a few miles east.

She could still not spot anyone that would match the figure she had followed. She halted. It struck her that the character she was chasing had nothing to look for in Harrods. In fact, his behaviour was not even of someone who had been made, but simply someone who was well accustomed to shaking off any potential tail.

She started running again towards the luxury accessories rooms, to the dismay of the bored security guys who started calling after her. There were at least ten doors to the ground floor so choosing the western ones was a gamble, but a good one as she was quite certain he would try to exit the building from its other end. She still wasn't quite certain about the guy's appearance, save the dark coat, but she thought his hair was fair or white. As she passed the front doors she took a left through the gloomy illuminated fine jewellery rooms. The displays were mesmerizing, with beautiful Bvlgari pendants and Tiffany rings glowing in a dark thin corridor. She kept her focus.

As she passed the fine watches and ran past the escalator leading to the wine shop, she entered the small L'Adurée café. The décor was marble white, and the floor was slippery. It appeared that the gamble had paid off as she caught a glimpse of a white-haired man dressed in a black UNIQLO coat exiting through the small outer door. His appearance was grim and he stood rigidly conspicuous in front of the colourful macaroons on display and the beehive of white shelves stacked with all kind of luxurious foods. There was no salesperson in sight, and as she ran straight after him, nearly knocking down the metal queue pole. She managed to balance herself and exited to Hans Road, the man was already turned towards her, a twenty-two millimetre Bobcat Beretta was visible in his hand.

"You?!" he exclaimed, quickly re-holstering the pistol. "You're Jensen's girl. What are you doing here?"

"Do we know each other?" She was perplexed. She recognized him from the rendezvous he had with John in

Mayfair the other night, but she could not understand from where he knew her.

"Had a chat with your boss yesterday. You were quite conspicuous there in Mayfair, really should be more alert, dear, not everyone you'll be following is a civilian like Mr Daniel."

She tried to protest but he went on. "You also don't want to be making such a racket when you engage someone who had no idea you were following him." He smiled. It was eerie. "If you weren't a woman I'd have blown your head off already."

She detested him straight away. It was chauvinistic remarks like that which got her all fired up. It was getting colder and a freezing gust swept through the small road, causing her to shiver. He had apparently been working with Jensen, but who was this guy?

"Where is he anyway? He wouldn't answer his mobile." His tone was curt and impatient, she felt like he was treating her as if she was one of his underlings. She swallowed down the feelings of insult when she suddenly realized this could work in her favour.

"I can't reach him either. Since this morning… well… the service is a mess."

"So you were assigned to make sure Grey keeps quiet then." It was more of a statement than a question. "What are your plans for the guy? Daniel?"

"He's not a problem. Scared shitless. With Grey out we're safe." She was improvising.

"Any word of Nikolayev?"

Was he testing her? She had no idea about Nikolayev, she had heard the name for the first time when she spoke with John earlier. "I have no information regarding him. I think that's where Jensen has disappeared to." Safe answer. If he was testing her, she gave nothing.

"If you reach Jensen, tell him my boss, the Minister, needs to know how to proceed. The Americans must know as well, either way."

It wasn't a test. This was running deep. Deeper than she thought. She had to keep him talking, but to her disappointment he was buckling his coat, ready to break contact.

"Wait!" she half shouted. "How do I reach you?"

He put his hand into his pocket. Was he going to draw the weapon again? Had she blown it? Was he onto her?

In a swift motion, he took out a business card and placed it in her hand.

"I want to hear from either you, Jensen or C himself first thing tomorrow."

She nodded, but he didn't wait for her answer and started walking away towards Brompton Road.

Liz Shaw stood desolated in the middle of the alley, the wind now so strong it blew dust into her eyes. Her service was bent, she now realized. *Samuel*, she read his name from the card, represented a foreign interest. Whoever he was, he nonchalantly fired away names that were the top brass of the service, indicating that they were part of some scheme or ploy. This had to be dealt with. She hailed a cab and texted John's number. 'On my way back. You were right. Go back to UCH now'.

Chapter 33
Babylon-on-Thames

Vauxhall Cross building was quiet at this time of night. As the black taxi pulled by the entrance to the multi-terraced structure, John could not help but feel like he had arrived to the entrance of some ancient catacomb. Yellow lights brightly glowed on the top dual chimney-like towers, and all through the top floor. Very extravagant for what should be a secretive building, he thought to himself.

John looked up as they went through the massive front gate, which was painted in a distinctive turquoise, to match the top glass windows. He was nervous. During the cab ride, Liz had explained how they were going to play it: during the day, the main door was controlled by a biometric system. But since the system was relatively new and not bug free (to say the least) it was not being used during night-time, in order to save on the required IT staff that supported running it. Since the night checks were manual, she would distract the night guard as John would use her access card to enter. She would then get herself in while he waited for her in the lift lobby. It worked like a charm. The night security guard was so busy returning Liz's flirtatious glances that he didn't bother checking John's features against the picture that had popped up on his screen. Meanwhile, Liz acted like her pass had gone missing. After a small chat, an exchange of phone numbers and a less-than-thorough ID check she was in. Easy.

The door to Jensen's office was less problematic. They had passed through her department's inventory desk, and there was still someone on duty that had let her sign in on an electronic door-key scrambler. The card was then put next to the reader on Jensen's office's door, and... *Hey presto!* The door opened.

They were in the dark office, barely distinguishing the chestnut table and cabinet from the grey wall-to-wall carpets. John pulled up the expensive ergonomic chair and switched on the computer.

"This is your show; you think you can hack in?"

"Well, unless there's some remote mainframe computer to which I can't access the BIOS, then the PC itself will be a walk in the park. For everything else I will need to download an algorithm from my company's server. I didn't intend to leave that kind of footprint that will implicate my firm, but since your guys stole my laptop I don't have a choice. The program itself checks all the possible options in milliseconds, as long as it's a known password protocol."

"English please." She rolled her eyes.

"It's essentially a superfast algorithm we developed for trading. In finance, a millisecond delay can make all the difference – some algorithms are useless if they cannot hit a price before everyone else."

"Not helping," she said impatiently.

He was already restarting Windows and entering the computer's Command Prompt.

"Sec, I'm just creating a new user."

Liz was staring at the blue screen, as part of her training she underwent a basic course in cryptology, but the changing screens meant nothing at all to her.

"Okay, we're in. Let me just download the algorithm."

"How is this possible again?"

"One specialty financial software we develop…" he said as he was clicking his way around the desktop, installing new programs and simultaneously opening existing ones "…is for algo-trading."

She nodded as he turned to look at her briefly before he continued to fiddle with the desktop.

"Algo-trading means that you define an algorithm, say for example you tell the computer to buy every stock option that its underlying stock had more than eight buy orders in the past three minutes, then the computer does it automatically for you – for *every* stock option out there. We're talking thousands of 'buy' orders in less than a few seconds. If your software is any good you will be first in the market to act, and your system would be less subject to flaws."

"Why would you want something like that?"

"Well, pretty simple really." He was still working on the PC as he lowered his voice, "Say you researched back, based on tens of thousands of stock data, and you reached a conclusion that whenever a specific stock rises half a per cent within half an hour, prior to that there were at least eight bulk buy orders for it, in the period of three minutes. So far okay?"

She nodded as he briskly turned and made eye contact before getting back to working on the PC.

"So, while as a person you don't have the ability to scan through all the stocks that are currently trading, look for all of these that have eight or more buy orders, let alone place the required orders – the computer can. And it can also place 'buy' orders on your behalf, if you wanted it to. So if we're working on thousands of stocks at the same time, with very large sums of money, it's enough to get our system ninety-nine point nine per cent accurate, using our algo-software. Going back to my example, if this half per cent per stock historical data was indeed pointing to a sure trading pattern, then with our superfast software, you will buy all the right stocks that act in accordance of the pattern you have identified, and make money. Here we are!" He pushed back and smiled a triumphant smile. "We're in."

"So easy?"

"It wasn't easy at all. I'm just good at what I do." He smiled again, this time with a sense of cockiness that she didn't initially think he possessed. Rather than put her off, she actually liked it.

Footsteps were heard behind the door. "Is there anyone authorized to be in Jensen's office?" a security guy asked.

"Neh, it's probably just mice. Let's go."

"I was sure I heard something," the other voice said.

"Trust me, you don't want to be in Jensen's office, mate, heard some guy got sacked for playing with some model he has there," his friend answered, as the steps seemed to grow more distant.

They both sighed in relief.

"In my line of work, a clandestine mission in the middle of the night is hardly the time for chit chat," she rebuked him.

"Oh bugger off! You asked!"

They both laughed silently, mainly from a sense of relief.

"Seems like Mr Jensen was quite busy. Let's see what we have here."

The material on Jamie's computer had disturbed them. Not only did Jamie Jensen handle the hunt for John and Grey personally, a fact that Liz was not aware of even when she was working for him, he also possessed some information regarding the suspected assailants of yesterday's murderous terrorist act. They could not understand where Jensen had received his intelligence from, there was nothing written in his records to indicate any source or any SIGINT data. Furthermore, they couldn't access any of the web based emails that were on his browser history: there was no username nor any details except the fact that he frequented both Gmail and Hotmail while encrypting the computer log. The fact that he could hide his action through software was also news to Liz. It reminded John of George Orwell's *1984*'s 'Telescreen', and the senior party members' prerogative to switch it off. It was apparent that Jensen was taking measures to cover his tracks.

***

They had gathered whatever they could into a folder and downloaded it to a disk-on-key. John didn't think there was anything interesting about the fact that Jensen used private web-based email accounts, but along with the computer encryption logs – Liz suggested that it would come across as incriminating enough for Wey to order the logs deciphered. They had called him as they exited the building, and he insisted upon meeting up with them already at that same night.

As they were walking north on the Vauxhall Bridge John took a look back at the ominous building, its robotic characteristics emphasized by the yellow lights. He then looked at the black water of the Thames, tracking back the reflection of the south bank buildings' spectrum of white, blue and yellow, as far as he could.

It was a quiet night, not a single car in sight, whereas generally this was a busy enough artery of the city.

Liz's phone started to ring.

"Yes," she answered coldly.

As the caller spoke she removed the phone from her ear and pressed the speaker icon.

"…Are you there?" He could make out Sammy's irritating deep accented voice.

"How did you get this number?" Liz shot back the question.

"This is immaterial, my dear; are you listening?"

"Go on," Liz said, her eyes immediately filling with hatred for the man.

"As I said, you weren't very truthful with me, Miss Shaw. I thought we were playing for the same team."

"Life is full of surprises."

"If you want to play games, I guess this chat is pointless…"

"Wait—"

She looked at John. He stared at her, catching the reflection of the night light on her gentle features. He nodded.

"What do you want?"

"A chance to talk, in person, exchange information before I run off, you know information is part of our tradecraft, let me know what you've got, and I will simply connect the dots for you."

"You just want to make sure we have nothing incriminating on you and your masters—"

"And what if I do?"

"Some of us have a conscience, unlike you!" John blurted as Liz was waving her hand for him to back off. It was too late.

"Ah, young Yochanan. I wasn't aware this had turned out to be such a love story."

He wanted to answer but Liz blocked him by moving the phone away.

"In any case, conscience has nothing to do with it, ask Miss Shaw over there about it. You two have wasted enough of my time. Tomorrow 7 pm, I'll be waiting for you for ten minutes at the Emirates Air Line cable car terminal of Royal Victoria. My next stop will be the airport. So if you want to know… I suggest you be there."

He hung up leaving the two in silence staring at the twinkling lights in the black horizon.

Joni Dee

Chapter 34
A house somewhere in Ar-Raqqah, Syria

It was night-time in Syria. The house where Jensen was being kept as a guest of 'Sheik Nick' was a dump. The rebel forces seemed quite taken with Nikolayev, hence the affectious nickname. Jensen was dishevelled. He wasn't used to being kept under such conditions. The place was blazing hot and there was no adjoining shower to the dump of a room they had placed him in, in fact there didn't seem to be any showers at all. It looked like the house was occupied by at least ten high ranking jihadi rebels, it was constantly guarded and the other Islamist factions who occupied this city were keeping their distance. It was peculiar, Jensen initially thought, since Ar-Raqqah had been considered the Islamic State's interim capital, he wouldn't have thought anyone else would be welcome there.

It was later that Jensen heard the word *hudna*, temporary ceasefire. Were the Jihadists there as IS guests? Are they planning on exchanging him for a ransom? Why is Nikolayev keeping him here? The thought of escaping crossed his mind, but with the raging Islamists practically controlling most of these lands, and the occasional Syrian offensive – he stood no chance on his own, let alone unarmed.

Nikolayev had taken his sought-after passport. He had never intended on keeping his end of the bargain, he saw through them all along. Drunk, he had told this to Jensen a few nights ago. Most rebels were zealot Muslims, who wouldn't touch a drop of alcohol if their life depended on it but the top brass were a different story. Being less scrutinized and allowed more privacy, the commanders indulged themselves every now and then. However, unaccustomed to booze and not knowing how to hold their liquor, they tended to get rowdy and aggressive. Jensen feared for his life for the first time in a long time.

He lay on the stinking mattress waiting for his supper. Essentially it was always hummus, pita bread and olives. As he listened to sounds of gunfire reaching him from a distance, trying to determine the weapon that had originated it, he started reflecting on how he got caught up in this mess. The idea initially came from the political top. Cocky Olly Jones, high and mighty king of intelligence. The details were left to Stamper, who was less than useless. Jensen saw the potential of contributing considerably to his pension fund from this little adventure. If only Nikolayev had played ball. He cursed out loud.

"We don't encourage the kids to learn those kinds of English words here." A shadow appeared in the door with a tray. It was Nikolayev.

"I've had enough of this, Vasiliy!" Jensen lashed out and in a swift movement flipped the tray from Nikolayev's hands. It fell with a noisy metallic thud which caused two large guys to immediately appear behind Nikolayev. He motioned them with his hand to stand down.

"I understand your anger," Nikolayev said. "Imagine mine when I realized nobody in Teheran was actually expecting me." He sneered.

Jensen gulped.

"So you see, I had to make some plans of my own. The boys here were all very generous, but that's because they see the potential of what I am going to do for them using your British passport, so much better than the Polish one you initially promised."

"It was I who took you from Moscow, set you up in Pakistan, then North Korea, you would have already been dead or working for some American nuclear plant in Idaho, testing hard water till you died of cancer! Surely this has got to amount to something!" Jensen nearly cried.

"Ah stop whining, Jamie; this debt was already paid a decade ago. You are a very wealthy man thanks to me."

Jensen's stare was directed at the professor. Nikolayev just confirmed what he suspected all along, there will be no talking his way out of this one, he would need to prove his value. But how?

"Don't worry, Jamie, you have not outlived your usefulness yet. I need you."

Oh? Jensen thought. Maybe he wouldn't die in this hellhole after all.

"Once you hear what I have in store for London, you'll realize that I can't pull this off without you."

It hit him. Nikolayev was planning to detonate a nuclear device, *the* nuclear device, in the West. In London! He was utterly insane.

"I won't do it, Vasiliy!" he protested.

"Oh you will. Otherwise—"

"What? You're going to kill me? Go ahead; I've already done enough things I am not proud of."

"I'm gonna do better. Some of our peers in the Islamic State are more than happy to take you off our hands, so they told us, when they heard rumours of your visit. We have a few more days as guests in their realm to conclude an agreement before we have outstayed our welcome. I'm sure you'll like it better over there, they are well known for their hospitality."

Jamie Jensen was lost for words. He knew that the Islamists would have a far worse fate planned for him before they'd allow him to die. The British government wouldn't negotiate with them. He had no choice but to cooperate with this lunatic, at least until he figured a way out. He moved his gaze to the window, hearing a blast not far away which startled him. He jumped back.

"Syrian government forces," Nikolayev commented, "they're getting close, aided by the silly Russians. That's what's left of the big CCCP and its corrupt regime." He cursed in Russian and spat on the floor.

Jensen turned his head to Nikolayev. "Why, Vasiliy? We've done well for ourselves."

"No, Jensen, while you were busy making money out of my talent, I was forced to watch the capitalistic pig of a world you guys created. And I swore in the past that the West would pay. What better way than to bring chaos and oblivion to your doorstep, who knows, maybe other groups would be inspired by us and the Armageddon the Christians love so much to fear will arrive in our time. Imagine that, Jensen and Nikolayev, the bearers of the Apocalypse in the name of Islam!" His laughter was pitched and irking.

Jensen stared into the eyes of his captor and saw nothing but madness and resolution. He knew there would be no talking sense to this guy. As he turned back towards the window there was another blast, this time closer. He could even see its orange hue lighting up for a split second the Ar-Raqqah skyline, which was otherwise pitch black. This time he didn't even flinch.

Chapter 35
Hampstead

It was early Monday morning when Matt Wey had sat down on Sir Richard Willoughby's expensive leather sofa in the Hampstead mansion house. The living room area was wide and luxurious with a typical very high ceiling. Sir Willow was already seated on the opposite matching single-seat sofa, and the Permanent Under-Secretary, a thin grey-haired man by the name of William Jenkins was already waiting in the seat beside him. C, otherwise known as Anthony Stamper, was hovering above the three.

The help, a dark woman of forty, dressed in dark uniform and a white apron, served coffees in a delicate china set, which she placed on the low green glass table next to a rare purple-yellow orchid.

"Well, naturally we didn't know exactly what Jensen was doing," Sir Willow addressed the Permanent Secretary, Stamper nodding in the background.

"With all due respect, sir," Wey intervened. "Considering the material we have that was, by the way, nearly impossible to retrieve from his computer, I find that hard to believe." His jawline was stiff and his voice deep with conviction.

"Well… We had some knowledge, naturally, but—"

"I was not aware of anything!" the Permanent Secretary protested. "Which makes this smell like a conspiracy in my book!" The others were outraged by his words, Jenkins was not known to have ever raised his voice above that of the incumbent minister.

"I have talked with Mr Jenkins in private yesterday as soon as this information reached me." Wey's tone was more conciliatory. "I believe him when he says he was outside the loop. But if you guys won't play ball I will talk to the leader of the opposition and the Attorney General directly if I have to. Someone will take the rap for this."

"All right all right, gentlemen, let's not get all worked up. There was a solid attempt to do what's best for Britain. Whether we knew or not is irrelevant, and Parliament should not be dissolved on the back of this… this glitch."

"I would hardly call it a glitch, sir!" Mr Jenkins practically cried. "You have worked outside your mandate, against our allies, and worst of all you made such a cock-up of it all that the repercussions will be grave for us all!"

"You're forgetting yourself, Jenkins!" it was Stamper who walked towards them from the big garden facing windows. "Your job is to enforce the government policy – not to make it." He reached out and took a cup from the table, and drank its black contents, now cold.

"If the policy is against the services' charter then it is well within my job to oppose it, sir! It is you who is out of order."

"Gents, please." It was Sir Willow intervening. "It is a delicate time, much more delicate then to allow the political system to be in disarray; what is it that you want?"

"Were you aware, sir, that there are traces of web based activity linking Jensen to extreme Muslim factions? I had his PC dismantled by the top IT guys in the service when I was presented with some of the evidence. For all we know the terrorist act of yesterday could be directly linked to you, Sir Willow."

"Now that is simply preposterous!" Sir Willow cried. Stamper, pacing back towards the windows, looked more nervous than ever.

"Nonetheless, if you want this to blow off as quietly as possible, you will all have to step down. Both you and the PM. The successor will have to be someone in your party that can keep it together and hasn't got this shit attached to him."

Sir Willow nodded. He knew when he was beaten.

"I will have to call the PM right away."

"I believe that is a wise decision, sir, whether he goes down quietly or not is up to him, though if the press finds out from some other source, we cannot help you."

"Where's your golden boy – Olly Jones?" Stamper snapped. "My sources have seen him with that reporter."

"I don't know. He was unattainable." Sir Willow's face was pale and it seemed like he aged a decade.

"Stamper, the last one you have to worry about is Olly Jones, you will resign effective immediately," Jenkins remarked.

"On whose authority?"

"Please, Anthony," Wey cut in. "Your fingerprints are all over this. Your computer is being checked as we speak by my IT guys. Take your pension and let's not drag this beyond what we need to."

"What about Nikolayev and Jensen?" It was Jenkins again.

"Yes, their threat would need to be dealt with," Wey agreed. "But we cannot be the ones behind that in a time like this; it will look like we're warmongering considering their now-traced location. Do you want me to talk to the Americans?"

Stamper hissed.

"I will do the cleaning," Sir Willow said. "The Americans are involved at some level. We need to make sure we speak to the correct people, we don't want a bloodbath in Langley on our account." He sounded deflated.

"Very well," Wey said. "I will leave the details to you gents, as long as we're on the same page here."

Stamper sneered.

"You will be lucky not to go to prison for what you've done, Anthony – I don't want to hear another sound from your end," Jenkins said.

"We'll convene in Whitehall at 8 pm tonight," Wey ordered.

"Sir Ainsley of MI5 will have to assume command of SIS, with no other vice chief, at least until a permanent replacement for Stamper will be appointed."

"I will put him in the thick of it; I expect the political arrangements would be dealt with by then," Wey said.

Wey and Jenkins stood up as Sir Willow kept nodding. His eyes reflected great sadness and he felt utterly defeated. He reached his phone and dialled a short number. "Get me the PM. Tell him this can't wait."

Chapter 36
The Emirates Air Line

The day had gone by placidly for John and Liz as they waited for Adam Grey to come round again. It was nearly dusk when they had arrived at Royal Victoria station. They kept Grey in the dark, he would need his strength, and worrying from his hospital bed would not serve any purpose, they had both agreed.

The ten minute Emirates Air Line cable car ride would allow them to talk privately with Sammy, and bug-free. They had to hand it to him, the old Mossad handler was extremely shrewd.

Earlier in the day the *Telegraph* had published headlines from an interview with Olly Jones, special advisor to the PM, which would be published next weekend. The headlines said that Jones had pointed a very accusing finger at the establishment, including the PM himself. He had acknowledged Britain's futile attempt to derail the nuclear talks with Iran, in shady ways. Some of the facts were accurate, but they revealed a very partial picture of what they had exposed just the night before when the information they gathered had indeed brought Matt Wey to raid both Jensen and C's computers. Though the service's involvement with terrorists was not confirmed nor mentioned, he implied that they possessed early knowledge of the terrorist attack and failed to act on it. The headlines were enough to enrage the masses. As a result, a crowd of people gathered in Westminster, demanding the PM's resignation. The protest had since picked up and a mob of a few thousand was already confronting police forces outside Downing Street and Parliament. The city was drenched in chaos.

As they walked towards the deserted pier, they could see the cable cars lit with a red neon stripe. The dark blue horizon was soon going to be black save the city lights and the Millennium Dome that was already brightly lit. They swiped their Oyster travel cards and walked up the escalator to the cable car floor, they were completely alone, as three empty cabins were slowly turning, waiting for a passenger to hop on.

"What now?" John asked.

"We wait," Liz suggested, as they saw the empty cabins leaving the docking station, gaining speed up the wire.

Another five minutes had passed in silence when they finally heard footsteps. "Miss Shaw! Mr Daniel!" Sammy's voice was unmistakably heard from the escalator. His usual grim presence was soon to follow. He wore a trench coat and a matching hat. His Beretta handgun was apparent in his left hand.

"You're not going to shoot anyone!" Liz exclaimed.

"Aren't I?" He smirked. Taking his aim at one of the very high neon lights from above and squeezing the trigger. The gun was equipped with a silencer, but the neon burst with a big thud. Shreds of white glass had fallen on Liz and John, landing on their coats. John sheltered his head, while Liz did not flinch.

"Get into this one and leave your firearms behind." He motioned them to an empty cabin that was just reaching the dock.

John took a glance at Liz who at her turn nodded, she crouched, put her Walther on the floor and the two got in. Sammy waited until they got to the end of the cabin, and jumped in at the last chance, just before the automated door closed behind him.

The cabin was going up, tilting heavily with the evening breeze, and the three sat in silence. John was pale, due to either the gun that was pointed at his direction or the constant shaking of the pod up high in the air. He had a bad feeling about it all. The cabin went past the first tower with a big crackling sound, when Sammy finally spoke. "You kids have really ruined it, you know?" He was waving his gun along as he talked.

"Now I'm a pragmatist. I don't care what you did and why you did it, it's out – we lost, I can only sulk and let you know that you helped make the world a far worse and scarier place. But having said that – I don't give a rat's ass. I need to think about what's next, and I simply can't allow you two to drag me into it. My so-called involvement will read badly with the Americans, with the world, with everyone."

"You've been manipulating everyone for too long, it's time you paid for some of the things you've done," Liz said.

"Righteous girl," Sammy scoffed. "So hard to find these days. I wonder if we would even be having this conversation if a bomb hadn't gone off in central London yesterday or you would have kept taking our orders silently and obediently." He sneered, enraging her.

John was oblivious to the conversation, he stared at the horizon. Despite the strong wind the night was clear and he thought he could see centres of light coming from Westminster, whether they were police spots or fire, again, he did not know.

The cabin reached the middle tower and a gust made it tilt heavily to the side. Sammy lost his balance and slid to the floor. Liz thrust forward and leaped onto him, in an effort to knock the gun from his hand. During the struggle a shot was fired and the bullet shattered the forward glass of the pod. The wind started blowing hard through the missing glass, and the cabin, still moving, was tilting and shaking rapidly.

"John!" Liz shouted as she was trying to pull her weight on top of Sammy. The wind was whistling inside the cabin, John jumped to his feet, adding more pressure on the heavily shaking cabin. By the time he got to Sammy he had already punched Liz across the face with the handgun, knocking her out. In the process of striking Liz, the firearm flew from his hand, and landed with a metallic bang on the other side of the cabin. It missed flying through the shattered window by inches. A big rumble was heard as the cabin went through the third tower, but both men were oblivious to the creaking and screeching noises. Had they taken notice, they would have probably stood still until the journey was up. Instead, instinctively, they both went after the pistol, leaping to the other end of the cabin.

John had reached the gun, but he felt the weight of Sammy's body pressing him to the side of the cabin, his knees pushed against the glass, while his torso stuck out of the broken window. Pieces of glass cut through John's body as he tried to shake the older man off. Sammy was powerful for his age, and John knew that he couldn't hold on much longer. Meanwhile the wind grew even stronger, whipping at them both, as the pod was already on its descent route.

They could see the docking terminal on the other side of the Thames, lit with the familiar bluish-neon lights. They were just on the edge of the Thames when John, with one great effort, managed to throw Sammy from above him. Sammy backed up and tripped over Liz who was still sprawled on the floor of the cabin, unconscious. He hit the side of the pod head first, with a big thud, which caused the automatic lock mechanism to fail. The doors were suddenly ajar. A big gust tilted the pod nearly forty-five degrees, causing Sammy to lose his footing; he flew out of the cabin. John ran towards the door and grip caught Liz's leg so that she wouldn't slide out. When the cabin finally stabilized he managed to force the doors closed and he climbed on the bench on the other side. He tried to look down to where Sammy fell to the Thames but the black choppy water revealed nothing at all. Abruptly, the scenery had changed and the dark night was replaced with the grey-metallic docking station.

The doors were now stuck, and he used force to get them to open. Liz was regaining consciousness and he helped her out before the shuttered pod turned and continued its trip back. As they stumbled on to the floor of the empty docking station she took one look at John, he was shaking hard and panting.

"Sammy?"

"I don't think we have to worry about him any more," he told her, sniffling, nearly sobbing.

He helped her to her feet and the two embraced.

Chapter 37
West Hampstead

Adam Grey walked slowly up West End Lane. His limbs were still weak and his arm limited in its mobility. But he was alive, and in relatively good shape. A week ago he was still lying in a hospital bed, and now he was back on his feet. Sooner than the doctors had anticipated.

They had advised him to stay home and recuperate – but he'd have plenty of time to do that when he's dead. His arm still needed massive physio work, and he knew that the road to being his old self was still long.

The cold night air was chilling and the streets remained calm. He walked past the everlasting construction site by the rail tracks, where a man wearing a beanie skullcap stood in the shadows and exhaled thick foggy purple cigarette smoke into the night. The pubs and bars were relatively busy in anticipation of the PM's press conference, scheduled for 9 pm.

Rumour had it that the infallible leader would announce his resignation today, and since the coalition was as fragile as it was, the act would force the dissolution of Parliament and the UK would be forced into new elections.

Having been filled in by Neil Finch as to what had occurred when he was out, Grey thought the PM's resignation and that subsequent scenario may very well happen. Probably some deal had been made behind the scenes keeping the real conspirators out of harm. Moreover, the *Telegraph* was advertising an interview with a senior governmental official, to be released tomorrow in the Sunday edition. A Katie Jones' exclusive. If Jones was involved it must be good stuff, he thought as he cleared past the West Hampstead Thameslink train station.

He reflected on a meeting that he held earlier that day in a shisha bar on Edgware Road. After learning the extent of Jamie's corruption, he concluded that it was unlikely that both Jamie's counter intelligence department and MI5 had completely missed the Tube's suicide bombing. Could there truly have been no leads? The terrorist act and the Nikolayev conspiracy overlapping was a rare coincidence that created a perfect cover for Jensen to get out of the country. He didn't believe in coincidences.

The only old devil that knew everything that went on in terms of Islamic terrorism, and incidentally helped stir at least half of it, was an agent only known as Marrakesh. Getting to the fiend was impossible. However, one of his cousins Ayman was a whole different story. In the height of the first Gulf War, Grey had smuggled Ayman and his family out of Kuwait, he had never collected back the favour.

"I cannot be seen with you, Adam," Ayman had said, as he exhaled apple scented smoke. He was holding the shisha's tube firmly and had motioned it towards Grey who had declined twice with a hand gesture.

"Me?" Grey had answered. "I'm a retired worn-down spook. An old man discussing the good old days with an old mate. Innit?" He had said while sipping from a bottle of an ice cold Peroni. He could never pass as a simpleton, it sounded fake.

"I don't have what you need."

"But what is it that I need?" He hated talking riddles with these guys, he always had.

"Marrakesh."

"Eeeeh!" he mimicked a gameshow buzzer sound. "Wrong!"

Ayman's inquisitive look was hard to overlook.

"There has been unproven and unidentified communication between an English man and Marrakesh."

Ayman had kept smoking the sweet apple scented tobacco.

"If this is wrong or you heard nothing of this – leave the table now."

Ayman had stayed put.

"It went from a private Hotmail account which we still can't access. Do you have anything to add? This will square your debt to me for good." He emptied the bottle and signalled the waiter for another.

"Don't get me wrong," Ayman said. "It was an ideological *Amaliya Intichariyae*." He used the derogatory Arab wording for suicide bombing, and not the term that means a heroic martyrdom act. This was an act of respect towards Grey, which did not go unnoticed. "Let's just say that Marrakesh also got paid handsomely for setting it up a few months ahead of schedule."

"I need a name."

Ayman had hesitated when Grey had aggressively grabbed his arm and had looked him straight in the eye. He whispered the name, "Jamil."

The information from Ayman had been immediately shared with Matt Wey, who in turn notified whoever needed to know. The footprint of Jamil was found on Jamie Jensen's computer, he was sure that they were the same man. Now, whether or not Jamie was found, was not his problem any more. Sure, he'd love a few minutes with him alone in a room, but that wasn't necessary. The main thing for him was to find Petr Haft and tell him he was safe.

Before crossing the street, he halted in front of West End Lane bookshop. He loved these little old bookstores packed with wooden bookcases, overcrowded with books; he was old fashioned, he conceded. He passed the already closed Indian restaurant, the spices and scents still heavy on the street corner, and he went inside the packed Alice House.

He found it hard to push through the small pub, as punters were standing pressed to the black bar itself, and every table outside was occupied. People were also standing uncomfortably between the tables and the place was very dark, making the walls seem dingier than the black night itself. The small hanging bulbs produced ambient light that was mainly an ornament and produced no illumination whatsoever.

It took Grey a while to deduct that he would find him here, but he attributed the slowness to the concussion he had suffered. The penny dropped the other day as he randomly remembered that Henry Haft had once made a 'mistake' and exposed a crack in his otherwise impenetrable armour of privacy. It was during a chat in the early 2000s that he had disclosed to Grey the existence of a certain 'lady friend' up in West Hampstead. It wasn't unusual for a source to confide in an agent of such things, nor was it anything particularly interesting. However, for the secretive Ephraim to let a personal detail slip was a major faux-pas back in the day.

Grey had assumed that Henry wanted to protect Petr, his son, at all cost. He had suspected that the paragraph in the letter about Petr's disappearance was not accurate, in an attempt to conceal his whereabouts in case the letter fell into the wrong hands.

Grey had always thought it was a good thing that sources' families and relatives had normally lacked imagination. There was no Petr Haft in West Hampstead, but there were only four Petr's in a very short proximity. A quick background check had eliminated three: two were married, one held a blue badge. This left a Mr Petr Bukowski, owner of a property on Iverson Road.

When you have eliminated the impossible, whatever remains, however improbable, must be the truth. It was an old Sherlock Holmes proverb. It still applied. So unimaginative, keeping his own name, not to mention using his mother's maiden name; an absolute folly. But it got him to Petr, and not anyone else ahead of him. That was the important thing.

He spotted a man who seemed to match the description he had for Petr, on the other side of the bar. He was sitting alone on a stool, there were no empty seats next to him but people were standing around him, engulfing him. Grey shoved towards him. It took some effort but he finally managed to stand right next to where he was sitting.

"Petr," he tried to say below the loud music.

"So you came for me," Haft responded, as he stood up from his slouchy stool sitting position. "I'm ready." He looked pale and frightened.

"You got it wrong, kid." He found himself shouting, his ears still hurting from the blast, oversensitive to the chatter and loud music which possessed the place. "I'm a friend of your old man."

Haft's features relaxed straight away. "How did you trace me?"

"Shall we talk somewhere quieter?"

Petr nodded. As he was about to move on, Grey signalled the now free barkeeper with his finger.

"Wait, let's have one for the road. What's your poison?"

"Vodka. Neat." Grey was afraid he would say that…

* * *

They walked in silence down the road. As the street turned to Abbey Road and the scenery became more residential, Petr finally talked.

"How did you find me?"

"If you want to stay low, don't go using your mother's maiden name and don't take refuge with your tenant in a flat that's owned by you, *capisce*?"

Petr nodded.

"You're lucky they didn't come for you."

"Who's *they*?"

Grey remained mute.

"He was murdered, wasn't he?"

Grey nodded.

Petr held his face with his hands and sobbed. "It was all my doing. If I hadn't done that thing with the passports—"

"But you did and it's done. And sobbing won't bring him back. Take comfort in the fact that you did what you did, and it got to your father's attention, otherwise who knows what these people would have gotten away with. In a sense a lot of good had come from his sacrifice."

Petr Haft raised his head and caught a glimpse of an ancient Gothic church on the left-hand side. He let his dark forelock fall to the side of his head and adjusted his spectacles.

"What now? Mr—?"

"Call me Murray." Grey had an unexplained grin. "I'm here to tell you that you can go back to your life, whoever's responsible for your dad's death will be punished. Those that directed him will no longer hold office. It's over."

Haft stood motionless, he was searching for words but was at a loss. Grey acknowledged his silence as gratitude, and hailed the first black cab that was wearing an orange vacancy light.

As the taxi drove down Abbey Road, it became stuck in a traffic jam in front of the famous studios, which hosted the Beatles back in the day. Grey, who was impatient to catch the PM's conference, pressed the driver's intercom button. "Any idea what's the holdup?"

The sound from the speakers had a metallic tang. "It's this damn zebra crossin', innit?"

As the cab crept passed the corner, Grey eyed a few tourists who were posing in the same manner as the iconic Beatles did, in spite of the darkness, creating a congestion. It made his mind wander to the seventies, when he was still in school. He'd met a few Jamie Jensens in those days; all grew up to be corrupt and influential, either in finance or in different areas. But would they be capable of mass murder just to cover up their tracks? He seriously doubted it.

"Any word on the PM's press conference?" he asked the driver over the intercom.

"They just announced it will be on later, didn't they?" the metallic voice answered. "Some urgent cabinet meeting is taking place first."

"Cheers," Grey replied. So it was on.

Chapter 38
Ar-Raqqah, Syria

The bombing above Ar-Raqqah's skyline ceased earlier that evening. The night was grey and pillars of smoke hung above the city. A small street lamp, which stood at the corner of the ruined house, was lit with an orange hue that was barely enough to cast a shadow on the barren ground. The house was buzzing all night with shipments, brought in dilapidated white vans.

Sleep eluded Jamie Jensen. He went out to what used to be a garden, for a smoke. As he lit his last Marlborough Gold he heard rustling from the direction of the main house. He inhaled deeply on the cigarette and exhaled a ring of smoke.

"You're enjoying it aren't you?" It was Nikolayev, stepping up to the small torch-lit wreck of a pavilion.

"Huh?" Jensen motioned to him and took another drag from the cigarette.

"The cigarette."

"Ahhh. Well what choice do I have? Besides, I'm down to my last one, so I'd better savour this before I'm compelled to switch to the local brand."

"You'd better just quit," Nikolayev laughed. "Besides, we're clearing off tomorrow, you'll have your precious Western cigarettes back soon enough."

"Where are we going?" He couldn't hide his relief from leaving this godforsaken place, especially since he wasn't at all sure that Nikolayev was going to be true to his word and keep him alive, as long as they're in 'Jihadi-land'.

"Patience, my friend; all in good time." Nikolayev grinned and lit a local branded cigarette.

***

The Cabinet Office Briefing Room A, also known as COBRA, was in full capacity. Aides, both ministerial as well as in uniform were roaming the outer corridor, as the wide oak oval table inside was occupied by some of the leading military and defence personnel in the land. Olly sat near an empty black leather chair at the head of the table, whereas on the other side of it sat Sir Willow, looking tired and as preoccupied as ever. The rest of the seats were full with high ranking generals, among them the General Chief of the Defence Staff and the First Sea Lord. Anthony Stamper was conspicuously absent, and the PM's chair between Olly and Willow was still empty.

"Sir, we have General Dempsey online," the Adjutant Captain said to no one in particular.

As the plasma screen showed the face of a solemn American General, the Chief of Defence Staff stood up. However, before he managed to say a word, Olly Jones leaned forward in his chair and called out loud, "General! Olly Jones here. So nice to have you with us; where are you currently controlling this mission from?"

The Chief of Defence Staff shot a chilling look towards Olly, but when the latter refused to acknowledge his gaze, simply frowned and sat down without drawing further attention.

"Our command post is not far from the border, on the Turkish side, of course, near a town called Gaziantep. Now, if we are done with geography lessons, I really need your chief to be present, these are my orders."

"He will be here any minute now," Olly said without appearing to have registered the insult. He knew the American general was a non BS kind of guy, a grumpy version of John Wayne even; hammering back was pointless. He would not proceed without the PM, and he would not allow them more than a few more minutes of delay.

"Gentlemen." The Prime Minister's low voice sliced up the tension in the room, as the attendants straightened up in their seats.

"Mr Prime Minister!" exclaimed General Dempsey, as if he had been waiting for someone else to appear.

"General," the PM nodded. "Let's make it quick, I've had a rough day and it doesn't seem to be getting any better." He sat down heavily.

"Mr Prime Minister," one of the aides from the side of the door called out. "We have the Oval Office on the line, sir, General Dempsey should just have received an authorization code—"

"I sure have, sir." The General's image swirled but the audio link was good.

"Olly," the PM looked to his right.

"Sir."

"Is the intel solid?"

"Yessir. We believe it is." Sir Willow nodded in assent, though the PM's gaze had not set on him even once since he had entered the room. Olly Jones hated reaching out to the Americans for military aid, it made the British look weak, albeit time was of the essence, and the American mission to the area was the closest and best to carry out the operation. Besides, it seemed best to let the Americans clean up, since there was a British national involved, yet no trial was conducted. Lord knows the Americans weren't shy from action, he thought to himself.

"Well then." The PM paused. "You have my go ahead and official thank you, General."

"With pleasure, sir." The General kept giving instructions in the background. "Captain Liu, the floor is yours."

Young Captain Yan Liu picked up her receiver and said a few inaudible words, she then turned to the General, ignoring the screen. "Operation Helping Hand is a go, sir. You will have a visual in a couple of minutes."

The General nodded.

"Thank you, General, the British government salutes you," the PM said with a voice heavy with authority then stood abruptly. "Willow, follow me, Olly – see this thing through."

"Yes, sir," he said as the PM and Sir Willoughby left the room.

***

The two F-35 Lightning mark II flew in perfect symmetry above the dark clouds, curving the black starry night with their piping jet engines. They were a dark work of art, completely undetectable by radar. If it wasn't for their yellow and orange tail marking and flickering lights, they would have been completely camouflaged.

As their interactive helmet signalled that the target bank had been loaded, each of the pilots armed their JASSM cruise missiles and lifted the safety off the right-hand trigger. They then rotated left in one swift yet smooth motion, and with a gust of thruster power – broke through the sea of clouds into the Syrian skyline.

As both pilots were positioning themselves perfectly at a thirty degree angle to Ar-Raqqah the com system had blasted in their ears the final approval. "Green light, boys, may God have mercy on their souls."

***

As he stubbed his cigarette with his shoe, Jamie Jensen heard the distant roar. He lifted his eyes towards the skyline and could see a bright orange burst on the horizon followed by grey smoke. The noise was deafening as the sky went from black to bright white. Then with one big ominous bang, it all went black.

Chapter 39
Regent's Park, December 1990

"It's over, Henry. Jaruzelski is resigning, Wałęsa will be sworn in within ten days. Last year the statue of Dzerzhinsky, the founder of the Cheka was torn down in Bank Square; did you think you would live to see this day? I'll say it again IT'S OVER, Henry, your fight is over. You can go home."

"Home, Mr Murray?" He turned to Grey and gave him a judgmental look, one that was always accompanied with a deafening silence of at least sixty seconds. Was he taking the time to arrange his words or was he deliberately winding him up? Grey had given up on finding the answer. "Home is where one feels he belongs, yes?" he kept his eyes on Grey. "I had not such a place for many, many years, sir. London is not my own, and Poland will never be my home again."

It was a bright and sunny day, but the sun produced no heat at all, a fact which didn't deter some children from running around the green in shorts. Otherwise people were out with heavy coats, as Grey and Ephraim continued their stroll along Queen Mary's rose garden.

"What will you do?" Grey asked.

"Well, Mr Murray," try as he might, he could not get Ephraim to call him Adam or Grey, "I have my small pension both from the service and the Polish government. Maybe I'll write my memoirs, or even start what you British call an investment portfolio." He chuckled, amused by his own little joke. In a decade of working together, throughout hundreds of meetings, it was the first time he had witnessed Ephraim actually capable of smiling.

"Seriously now, Henry, will you be alright?"

"You said it, Mr Murray: the Iron Curtain is indeed singing its swan song. *The wolf also shall dwell with the lamb, and the leopard shall lie down with the kid; and the calf and the young lion and the fatling together; and a little child shall lead them.*"

"King James' version?"

"You know your Bible, Mr Murray, I'm impressed. Isiah eleven: six to be precise."

"Your idea of sarcasm, Henry?"

"Spot on, Mr Murray."

"So you don't believe we're on the verge of peace and harmony to the world?"

"And the wolf shall dwell is the only part of this sentence I can be coerced to support."

"Meaning?"

"There are wolves among us, Mr Murray. The world is on the edge of the abyss. The unknown. They will pop up like mushrooms after a rain, will try to profit from the chaos."

"And you?"

"I will be here. Waiting. Watching."

They turned right, passing through the big black and gold embellished gates. A taxi was waiting for Grey with the engine running.

"That's my ride, Henry." He pulled a dossier from his inner pocket. "A little something to show Her Majesty's appreciation for all you have done. It comes with a small grant, nothing too exciting, but enough to get you a nice holiday somewhere warm. You earned it, Henry, much more than that."

The older man accepted the Certificate of Merit and grasped it firmly, Grey was afraid he would rip the paper.

"Can I give you a ride anywhere?" Grey asked affably.

"I'll be alright, Mr Murray. You just keep fighting the next war, whatever it may be."

"Well, I'll see you around, Henry, it's been a pleasure." He reached out his hand, which Ephraim didn't take.

"It had indeed been a pleasure, sir, but this is goodbye, Mr Murray. I doubt we will ever see each other again."

Grey nodded, acknowledging defeat. Each man had turned his back to the other, and while Ephraim doubled back towards the gardens, Grey was making his way to the black cab. As he sat in, he realized that there were many more questions he would have wanted to ask Henry Haft. As he rolled down the window, he could no longer spot him between the flower beds. He thought about calling after him, but the cab shot off and sped down the road.

Chapter 40
Ar-Raqqah, Syria

"*Ta'al Ta'al. Bring the stretcher – there's a live one here!*" A heavyset man was calling in Arabic to his friends, who were busy moving rubble with their hands. Their search and rescue mission had started in the midst of the night, and so far they had managed to retrieve five bodies and one badly wounded survivor. This new one was spared by being caught in an air pocket that had formed between two collapsed storeys of the house. Most of his wounds were superficial, save an open fracture of a leg. His lungs sustained the majority of the damage as he inhaled dust and particles. He was reached by the first responders moments before he would have suffocated. It looked like Allah was guarding this one personally.

They seated the man upright, and covered his legs with a scruffy blanket. Before the stretcher could be found, a dark moustached doctor had arrived, armed with a stethoscope. He was sweating heavily in his short sleeved dress shirt.

"*His vitals are fine,*" the doctor announced in Syrian Arabic to the smiling faces of the rescue men. "*Superficial wounds and I guess a deep state of shock. His leg will need surgery and a cast, but nothing life threatening, Allah be blessed.*"

The man eyed him. He was covered with a thick layer of dust and sweat, and was salivating.

"*Drink!*" the burly man who had found him initially commanded, as he forced a metal canister full of warm water towards the survivor's mouth. He drank the foul tasting water longingly.

"*Kif sar?*" what happened. The man asked in a hoarse voice.

"*Tayarat*" airplanes. The rescuer answered. One of the crowding people had emulated a jet with his palm and 'flew' it with his arm raised high.

"What is your name, brother?" the physician asked in perfect English.

"Me?" The man seemed perplexed by the question. The burly man and the doctor both nodded in anticipation. "I don't remember."

"Come, brother, let's get you on the ambulance. You need to be properly checked and bandaged in the *mustashfa*... erm... hospital."

He was sitting in the back of an old dusty Red Crescent ambulance, with the badly wounded man lying on a stretcher on the floor of the vehicle. He tried reflecting on last night. He remembered the jets and the burst of fire, but he couldn't remember what he had been doing before that, or what happened next. He couldn't be sure how he had survived, but he was certain that the attack was aimed at him and the professor, and not coincidental.

He started sweating hard in the inside of the stuffy ambulance, as it drove frantically between the sandy neighbourhoods. "Indeed I have no name now," he muttered to himself below the agonizing cries of the wounded man. "Jamie Jensen is dead and buried."

Epilogue: John

It was a glorious day. The sun was up with all her might, covering London with a blanket of yellow rays that rapidly dissolved the morning mists. He awoke late. It was the first night in ages in which he managed a long lavish uninterrupted shut-eye. His head mildly ached, but it was a good headache, one that comes from oversleeping and would soon vanish with the morning coffee.

He was wearing a light black UNIQLO windbreaker, the chilly morning air felt refreshing against the exposed skin of his face. The city seemed different. Calm. The resignation of the PM a fortnight ago, along with the newly assembled parliamentary investigation committee seemed to have restored the public's assurance in the British democracy. The scheduled date for the dissolution of Parliament and the subsequent elections had taken the edge off of the opposition's call for action. It was as if the city's buildings themselves were gasping in relief.

John had met with Liz Shaw only once since that night at the Emirates Air Line. She was cold and distant, as if the events of that night had never even happened. He was okay with it though. If Liz Shaw wanted to play games – she could do so without him. He had read an article about this behaviour: people who tend to be in full control all the time, suffer a collapse of their reality after they feel like they owe their lives to someone else. She needs to get over herself, he thought.

Before arriving at the staircase that led up to Broadgate Circle, he halted. He looked up the big shapeless bronze statue: it was lifeless and rusty, and made no sense to him at all. His gaze then wandered behind his shoulder to the old cheese shop. He had never given it the time of day, but now remembered he had read a story in the paper about it. It was apparently affiliated with the suicide bombing on the Central Line. The police had raided it last week, and the shop's security shutter was closed shut ever since.

His mind kept leapfrogging and his chain of thought ended with Adam Grey. As he started climbing the stairs he couldn't help but wonder to himself what was the old spymaster doing. He last saw him in UCL Hospital, and he had not heard back since. He should have been discharged from the hospital at least a week ago. He thought about calling to check up on him and immediately dismissed the idea.

He walked into his regular Starbucks kiosk, exchanged pleasantries and a bit of affable banter with the staff who already had his triple espresso ready. He accepted the drink with a smile and started walking towards the office. Half-way there he decided to step into the Australian coffee shop and grab a pain-au-chocolate. Theirs was better. He would allow himself this small indulgence today, he deserved it.

He welcomed the routine. He missed it. He couldn't take another week like that one. At least he didn't think so. Mr Wey had awarded him a Certificate of Appreciation of some sort, and even mumbled something about an official ceremony at Buckingham Palace later this year. He hadn't heard from him since.

As he traversed Broadgate Circle he noticed a man who didn't quite fit in. He wasn't one of the City rats, who were rushing lemming-like to work, that much was apparent. He had a placid posture that seemed overly familiar. He couldn't make out his features but he was wearing slick skinny blue jeans and a black blazer. He was drinking coffee out of a takeaway cup.

As John drew near him, the man looked up and faced him. To his surprise Adam Grey was wearing his usual smug smirk, his slightly wrinkled face looked more rejuvenated than ever. He threw his cup to a near bin and put his arm on John's shoulder. He smiled and said, "Ready, kid? We've got a lot of work to do."

Afterword

Writing a book is hard. Publishing a book is just as hard. This book has taken me a few good years to write and a challenging year plus to get published. After you took the time to dive into John and his world, I thought you deserved a few words that will try to tackle some issues that may arise from this novel.

In spite of being a work of fiction *And the Wolf Shall Dwell* directly handles terrorist acts and the intelligence community's attitude towards them. The first issue that arises from the novel is its portraying of a suicide bomb attack going off in the London Underground. The moral dilemma whether or not to publish such a scene weighed heavy on my heart. Is it irresponsible to demonstrate a way of performing such an atrocious act (even though not lesser dreadful ones were already committed in London on 7/7/2005 and in Manchester on 22/5/2017)? Is it equally atrocious to implicate a character working for the British intelligence services in issuing the order for such an act?

While the answer to the latter question is that it's a matter of personal taste, the answer to the former one is something I had thought hard about. I can philosophically debate here for pages over pages that I have demonstrated nothing new, and that anyone driven enough to carry something as terrible as described – will find a way regardless of whether or not I had written it first, the evidence are the series of individual terrorists acts that are being carried in London nowadays. To address the issue, I'll use a free translation to an old Hebrew proverb: "reality surpasses any possible imagination". With today's atrocious worldwide attacks, it took me quite a few drafts to even devise a scene that would be able to top the sad everyday images we are accustomed to now. Anything lesser than the gruesome scene which Adam Grey wakes up to at the beginning of Book II, simply wouldn't 'cut it', nor could it have given the desired concussion effect. I was trying to rattle you, the reader, and if some of you are annoyed with me, well then – at least it worked.

As a kid, growing up in terror stricken Tel Aviv of the nineties, things were just as horrible. While I see my childhood as happy and normal, my friends and I could not go out to a club without the fear of blowing up in the queue, not to mention that attacks on coffee shops and explosions in bars became almost part of the quotidian life. So no, sadly in 2017, even such a scene could not top our reality.

The second issue, is it irresponsible to 'humanize' the terrorist attacker? Did I not go over the top giving Ahmed such an elaborated background that some readers may relate to? For me, the answer is unambiguously No. The reality, in which we live, is the product of the reality we create. Ahmed, albeit cruel and vicious (I especially found it hard to write the scene where he was staring with tearful eyes at the little girl next to him), had found a way to self-justify his acts. In his own distorted mind he's a martyr and in a way a victim no less than the people he will eventually murder. It is the murdering monsters who sent Ahmed that I could never help 'humanize' while they are knowingly taking advantage of the weak, and people in distress (whether spiritually challenged, in economic need, etc.) and reward them or their families for spilling the blood of innocents. Ahmed is no saint of course, he's a murderer of innocents, but the predicament that led him to this act ought to be mentioned.

Lastly, let me just proclaim that *And the Wolf Shall Dwell* is a work of fiction. All functionaries or departments, whether Israeli Mossad or MI6, are figments of my imagination and should be treated as such. Any resemblance to real life is coincidental at best, or plain lucky!

Acknowledgments

This book would have never seen the light of day if it wasn't for the help and support of a few people, to whom I wanted to thank specifically. This does not diminish the contribution of other people who had worked hard editing, designing and marketing *And the Wolf Shall Dwell* – to whom I thank profoundly even though I did not mention them by name.

This book was initially Crowdfunded, so first of all thanks to my family and friends, and to some of my parents' close friends who helped with the campaign, and accepted my nagging with love. Also, thanks to some new friends I've made, these people supported me just because they read a book they liked, most of them brilliant authors on their own merit.

A big thank you is due to Micha Knopf, who put in massive efforts to correct my English. And thanks to my editor Helen Baggott, who has done wonderful work correcting a mishmash of American, British and 'Israeli' English.

A huge thanks also to a very special guy, who's a fantastic author, and now runs his own publishing imprint. He decided to take a chance on me when I was down, and helped me throughout the entire publishing process – Olli Tooley.

A special thanks to my parents Yosefi and Mira as well as to my sister Michal, who pretty much support me in anything I try to do, with no reservations. The same thanks are due to my late grandma Savta Dvora, who from the knitting session at my nursery to the very end, had said Amen to pretty much anything I had said. I love you all very much.

Finally, a loving thanks to my children for being my inspiration and to my wife Yael who supported me throughout the process, including during the (very exhausting) Crowdfunding campaign. It's not easy Crowdfunding a book and can get stressful and hectic at times ranging from plain happiness to total despair. She stood by me through it all, and helped me actively. I love you all very much.

Last but not least, thank you the readers, whether you pre-ordered and helped me make this book a reality, or just picked up your copy. Without you John, Grey, and Co. would have only lived in one man's head. So thank you from the bottom of my heart. John will return!

> Sincerely,
> Joni Dee
> London, UK. 2017

Patron List

This book was made possible partially thanks to the generous help of the following patrons:

Arik & Yona Dotan
Ayelet Metzger & Family
Bernie and Dieda Robins
Daniel Goldberg
Daniella & Tibor Ritter
Diego and Anna Salazar
Dina Ruth
Hana & Yermi Negri
Herzel & Ilana Shalem
Imri Barzilai
Josl Pultuskier
Liora Shani
Maya Rozenman
Michal & the Shavit Family
Michal & Barak Rinat
Michel Mizrahi
Nigel Halligan
Nurit Rubinstein
Yael & Kobi Englender
Yayo & the Friedman Family
Yosefi & Mira Dital
Yoseph & Orit Rozenman
Yossi Menashe
Zvi & Shifra Yosipovitch

Also available from Blue Poppy Publishing

Children of the Wise Oak – Oliver J Tooley

As Blyth approaches manhood in the Celtic village which is all the world he has ever known, he dreads warrior training. All he wants is a quiet life. When his father returns from distant lands, instead of giving him a more settled family, events forced him and his two brothers to flee from home.

Taken under the wing of the powerful 'Deru-Weidi' mages, their journey leads them across a continent and their adventures force them all to grow up more quickly than warrior training would ever have done.

Black Lord of Eagles – Ben Blake

Imagine if, for three thousand years, your people believed they were the only people in the entire world… How would you face a sudden invasion? With your world-view turned on its head, how would you find the strength to resist?

The Ashir thought they were all alone in the world – until the strangers came. The invading Thrain have weapons of strange metal and ride beasts they have never seen before.

They have come to conquer. Anyone who opposes them is killed. The Ashir gather to fight, but it soon becomes clear that their only hope lies with one man. Kai, the kamachi, living servant of the Teacher God.

Kai has never heard the voice of his God, as kamachi are supposed to do. He doubts himself, despite the adulation of the people. But now he, and the only two men he trusts, must stand up to lead the resistance against a terrible enemy with no mercy in them.

www.bluepoppypublishing.co.uk

Printed in Poland
by Amazon Fulfillment
Poland Sp. z o.o., Wrocław